Gate Crasher
&
Other Stories

Gate Crasher
&
Other Stories

by

Frances Cherry

Earl of Seacliff Art Workshop
Paekakariki
Aotearoa, New Zealand
2006

© Frances Cherry 2006

Cover artwork: *One Morning* (2003) by Seraphine Pick
    oil on canvas   300 x 230 mm
    courtesy of the Artist and Michael Lett, Auckland

Back cover: Photo by Vivienne Joseph

Edited by Janet Secker

Typeset and designed by Brian E Turner

Printed by Crystal Clear Copy Shop, Otaki

Published by:

    Earl of Seacliff Art Workshop
    PO Box 42
    Paekakariki
    Aotearoa, New Zealand
    E-mail: pukapuka@paradise.net.nz
    Web site: www.earlofseacliff.co.nz

    ISBN 1-86942-056-X

Acknowledgements

Stories in this collection previously published:

An Evening Out in '100 NZ short short stories' - Tandem Press 1997 (as *Dragging It.*)
The Gift of a Son and *Waiting For Jim* - in 'The Daughter-in-Law and other stories' - New Womens' Press 1986.
Waiting For Jim also published in 'A Collection of Fiction by NZ Women 1870s - 1980s', ed Trudi McNaughton, Century Hutchinson 1989 (as *In Deadly Earnest.*)
Commos in 'Short Stories from New Zealand' selected by Alistair Paterson - Highgate Price Milburn 1988.

Dedication

To my father.

Dad, I remember your
cold dead face
on that white satin pillow
as if an artist had sculptured you
in wax

I watched your face afraid
to touch in case
the sound was hollow

Did I see an eyelid move
the flicker of a smile?
are you going to sit up
and laugh?
don't be silly, Francie
I was only kidding

Will you be back in that chair
beside Mum
knocking your pipe into your hand
flecks of tobacco all over
the floor
telling your stories

While Mum raises her eyes
to the ceiling and sighs
and we hope you
don't notice

In your face like
a speeded up film
I see myself and Maureen
you a stranger back from the war
our house in Rongotai

Neighbours, Communist Party
meetings, room full of smoke

You driving the trams
us bringing cheese and onion sandwiches
tea in a milkbottle with a
cardboard lid
down to the corner of Mamari Street

There were so many things
I wanted to say, Dad

Contents

In a Nutshell 11
The Lassie From Lancashire 13
Olga 15
The Gift of a Son 28
Owen 35
Letter From America 39
Gate Crasher 48
Waiting For Jim 60
A Cup of Tea 67
Mum and Cassandra 74
Jesus in the Shed 80
Inside Out 87
Overseas Experience 90
Wanting 97
Commos 103
An Evening Out 106
Betrayal 108
The Body 110
She's My Everything 116
Days of our Lives 118
French Farce 123

In a Nutshell

As soon as I saw him at Nola's place it was as if the air sizzled. I said to my sister when we were going home, 'I don't like him.' But he kept coming around and one time, after a party at our place, he took me on his motor-bike for a ride. It was early morning and there was no-one else on the road. We flew down Constable Street, me with my feet sticking out.

We went to the place he boarded at and ate rhubarb and weetbix for breakfast. He said, 'When we're married and you're forty, you'll probably be fat.' I was indignant about that but I liked the marriage bit because I had that inevitable feeling as well.

I felt as if I'd known him all my life.

I remember his brown arms and his white rolled-up shirt sleeves, the way he chewed a match when he was trying to give up smoking.

We had a white wedding in a church, even though I was pregnant and didn't believe in God. Then we went to a place called the Portage in the Marlborough Sounds. It was beautiful. He played pool and drank beer with the bloke who looked after the grounds while I lay on our bed feeling sick and, I must admit, a bit let-down. It wasn't what I had expected.

I was twenty.

We lived in a dark basement flat up a really steep hill and I thought, what now?

He worked as a Wool Presser in the Wool Stores and his hands were smooth from the lanolin.

He had a big birthmark on his inner thigh.

He cuddled me in bed at night and we talked and talked.

I was alone when I had the baby, my feet in stirrups, while an Irish nurse hissed in my ear to keep quiet.

He held the baby up in the air and said, 'I can't imagine loving any more children. I've only enough love for him.'

We had four more children and lived in a big expensive house out on the coast. He joined the Rotary Club, played golf and spent a lot of time in the pub.

I kept telling myself I was lucky.

When I was forty my eldest son said, 'Why don't you leave him?' And for the first time I realised I wasn't the only one being affected.

I'd got my own life without him being aware of it. He didn't like that and found another woman to love and make him feel needed. I knew when he came back from a golfing weekend that something had happened because his eyes were all dewy and he was so nice to me.

She even arranged a holiday for us all in a little house on the wild Wairarapa Coast when I was at the stage of sometimes thinking he was having an affair and sometimes thinking he wasn't.

He ended up with another woman, not her, and I ended up in a beautiful house overlooking the harbour where the kids and I had a lovely life with no-one to come in at the end of the day to spoil things.

Then he died at the age of forty-six and I felt as if someone had thrown a concrete block into my diaphragm.

Sometimes, now, I wish he was alive so I could tell him about computers, the internet, fax machines, cell phones. He'd be gobsmacked. I want to tell him, Mum and Dad died, that his children have grown into wonderful human beings, that he has lovely grandchildren.

I want to know if one day he might have understood.

The Lassie From Lancashire

She sits in that chair staring at her knees, she is on her soapbox again, *the workers must take over the means of production,* racing through a swirling past of political meetings, friends, neighbours and comrades. Dad there, young and handsome, - 'People never understood what he saw in me'.

She and Dad sitting in their chairs beside each other, that's how I remember them. Her reading the paper to him while he presses tobacco into his pipe, flecks falling onto his trousers and around his slippers. Her slamming the paper on to her lap, digging her fingers into her scalp. 'If I had my way I'd line them all against a wall and shoot them.'

I look at her thin bony hands, the wedding ring loose on her finger. Her watch swings around her wrist like a bracelet. She used to be such a buxom woman, breasts warm and soft to a child's head. Now there's nothing there. Even her teeth move in her mouth when she speaks. My mother is disappearing.

'Apart from your own home, this couldn't be a better place,' she says. They give me breakfast in bed every morning. Toast, porridge. They're very good. And, of course I'm very good to them. The woman in the next room,' she gestures with her head. 'I keep an eye on her when the matron goes out, get her back into bed when she falls out. I must save them thousands of dollars.'

'That's great, Mum.'

'Did I tell you the Duchess of York came to see me?'

'No, Mum.'

'Do you know,' She eyes me intently. 'She didn't know the song, *The Grand Old Duke of York?* So I sang it and her secretary wrote it down.' She smiles at her knees again. 'Paul's building me a house,' she says. 'He's a millionaire, you know, lives in France.'

'I don't think so, Mum.'

'Oh yes, he does. He told me.'

'The last time I saw him he lived in Sydney.'

'Well, he doesn't now.' She looks up at me, her beady eyes defying me to disagree with her.

'Is that so?'

'He's always liked *me*, always kept in touch. Your father's nephew but he's always kept in touch with *me*.'

'How will you live in this house? Who will look after you?'

'There'll be servants, of course.' She looks at me as if I'm an imbecile.

I notice the glasses hanging around her neck are caked with food.

'A man half my age,' she says. 'Wanted to marry me. I didn't trust him when his daughter brought him to see me so I had my lawyer here as well.'

'Why was that, Mum?'

'He's started a chain of fish and chip shops,' she says indignantly. 'Wanted my secret recipe.'

*

'I don't want to die,' she says. 'I don't want to be nothing.'

*

I look at my ankles and think of her ankles. I wear her wedding ring and her old red dressing gown.

Olga

I was surprised to see Nigel singing at the funeral of my friend's husband. I hadn't seen him for years, not since we'd been on that overseas trip. The three of us, him, me and Olga.

Afterwards when we were having a cup of tea I looked out for him through the crowd of people. He was talking to a member of the family. I stood by politely until he was free and then went up to him. 'Hello Nigel,' I said. 'I heard Olga had died. I'm sorry.' Luckily they'd had a small private funeral and I hadn't had the dilemma of deciding whether I should go or not.

'You know what happened, don't you?' he said.

'No.'

'She killed herself.'

'What?' I nearly fell over with shock.

'Come outside,' he said. 'I don't want all these people to see me cry.'

I followed him through the crowd to a sunny spot by the gate. 'Why Nigel?' I asked. 'Why would she do that?'

'She hated being old and unable to do what she wanted.' Tears trickled down his cheeks. 'I came home to find her with a plastic bag over her head.'

'Oh Nigel, that must have been terrible for you. How simply awful.' And then I asked, 'How old would she have been?'

'Ninety-one,' he said. 'Ninety-one.'

'Goodness,' I said. 'It must have been thirteen years ago when we had our trip. I hadn't realised how much time had gone by.'

'I so miss her,' he said.

'I'm sure you must. I know she meant a lot to you.'

'I loved her,' he said.

'Yes, I know.' I remember thinking, as I watched them walking ahead of me in Munich, her clutching his arm and snuggling up to him, that their relationship was like a sexless marriage.

I knew their story. Nigel had come into Olga's life when he was a very young, shy, homosexual man, ashamed of his sexuality. Olga, old enough to be his mother, had given him confidence and stability. They shared the same interests, music, singing, going to concerts and plays. Olga was a provocative, clever woman who had come from a strict religious background. I suppose you could say she was a bit of a shit-stirrer. She loved having an opposing opinion from everyone else. But not always. She'd been very kind to me and was exactly the person I needed when I was leaving my unhappy marriage. She was black and white about things – and sometimes you need that when making life-changing decisions. I liked her. I found her stimulating.

Eventually she and Nigel shared everything, the house, car and holidays. It was puzzling but nice. Takes all sorts, as they say. Nigel had his own lounge area downstairs for entertaining his friends. I remember his one serious relationship with Keith who he got on really well with – except that Olga went everywhere with them as well and, finally Keith couldn't stand it any more. He told me that when I bumped into him at the pictures.

I'd known Olga since I was a child. She'd lived in the next street to us. She had the same political leanings as my parents and was great friends with them. She had a son, who I quite fancied. His name was Lenin (which he changed to George when he was old enough). Olga expected a lot from that boy and insisted he read great literature, Tolstoy, Dostoevsky, stuff like that.

I found Olga fascinating. She had lovers, as well as having been married three times. That seemed so daring and exciting in those days. None of her relationships lasted. She had huge fallings-out with everyone, except my mother, who was the sort of person you couldn't fall out with.

Olga 17

'You know, Nigel,' I said. 'Olga liked having control, and she had it at the end. That's something.'

'Yes,' he said. 'I guess that *is* something.' He seemed comforted by my words.

'She wasn't easy,' I said. 'That trip was hell for me.'

'Yes.' He looked at me sympathetically. 'She said, only weeks before she died, that she knew she had destroyed most of the friendships in her life.'

'That's sad; but true.' I touched his arm. 'Do come and visit. I'd love to talk to you over a meal.'

'I will,' he said, and gave me a kiss on the cheek.

*

I'd often wondered over the years if I should try and make it up with Olga. But I just couldn't. I'd tested my feelings by asking myself what I would feel if she died and I'd decided I'd feel okay. I did.

*

I'd been really taken-aback when Olga rang me one day and asked if I'd like to go to Madrid with her. She was going on a Spanish Language tour with a group from Auckland University. We'd be there for a month before she and I, if I agreed, continued by Eurail around the rest of Europe for three weeks. 'I'll pay for everything,' she said, knowing I was on a benefit. 'Money means nothing to me. All you need is your own spending money for little things you might want to buy.'

When I hesitated she said, 'I'd really love you to come. We'll have a great time.'

'But you usually go away with Nigel.'

'He has to work so I thought I'd ask you instead. Please think about it.'

I felt in quite a state when I got off the phone. Should I go? What about the kids? Then I thought the youngest could stay with my mother, and the others, who were old enough, could look after themselves. That was, if I went. Was it a wise thing to do? And then I told myself that if I was Olga, and could afford it, I'd do the same thing. So I said, yes.

It was so exciting for me because I'd never been overseas before – except to Australia, which you can hardly count. It all went pretty well, meeting the rest of the group in Auckland and then flying on to Frankfurt, where we spent the night before going on to Madrid.

On the plane Olga told me that Nigel didn't know she was paying for me and please not to say anything to him.

Our hotel in Madrid was rather spartan and extremely cold. Olga made many complaints to the management but, for me, just to be on the other side of the world was wonderful.

I must say I was surprised when Olga said, as she was unpacking her bag, 'Oh dear, Nigel forgot to pack my shower cap.'

There were three of us who weren't actually studying the language on this tour so, while the others went off to their lessons every morning we visited art galleries – until Olga got tired of them and wanted to shop instead. The other woman was Coral, a tiny bird-like creature who was a heavy smoker, which was lucky for her because everyone, it seemed, smoked in Madrid. It turned out, so Coral told me, that Olga had suggested she come on the trip as well. I hadn't known that and was astonished that Olga hadn't said anything. Coral was always in front of us, as we left the hotel each morning and manouvered our way down the narrow cobblestone street, past cars that were parked parked haphazardly this way and that. Olga would criticise the way Coral walked. Everything about Coral seemed to annoy Olga for some reason. I wondered why Olga had suggested Coral come on the trip.

In the afternoons we went with the rest of the group to various areas of interest around Madrid. On weekends we had full day trips. Sometimes Olga didn't want to go and stayed back in the cold hotel reading, in bed.

We had our own favourite restaurant that we went to every night. We were always the first customers at 8pm because we never really got used to eating so late. All in all, I thought we got on pretty well.

It surprised me that Olga and Nigel talked on the phone every night. I hadn't realised, until then, just *how* close they were.

The longer we were in Madrid the more I worried about how we would get on when we had to organise our Eurail journey. The tickets were paid for but we had to decide where to go, where to stay – and book. I'd begun to realise that Olga wasn't good at things like that. And, she had no sense of direction. It would be up to me, and I felt quite nervous.

When Olga came into the room one night, after talking to Nigel on the phone, she said, 'Nigel's going to join us in Frankfurt and come with us around Europe.'

I was so relieved I could have hugged her. 'That's great,' I said.

*

When we get to the airport at Frankfurt he is there in his little blue and red cap waiting for us. Olga rushes up to him and throws her arms around him. They hug for quite some time, while I wait for my turn. But Olga just takes his arm, and off they walk, ahead of me. I am surprised but tell myself they are just so pleased to see each other.

When we get to the hotel Nigel tells us he's booked the train travel and that after a day in Frankfurt we'll be off to Heidelberg for three days. He tells us the other places but I can't quite take it all in, and I don't care where we go. I just feel so lucky to be going anywhere.

All the while he is talking Olga doesn't look at me. I tell myself she is just tired, and overwhelmed to see Nigel again.

When Nigel says to me. 'I've booked cheap hotels by the railway stations. It shouldn't cost us more than about 40 marks each, that is if we all share the one room?' He turns to Olga. 'Okay with you?'

'Fine,' she says. And she still doesn't look at me.

I don't know what to do. How can I afford to pay for the accommodation? But, maybe, Olga will talk to me about it later? Yes, that's what she'll do. She doesn't want Nigel to know, that's all.

We go to the railway station across the road for a meal. The railway station has many restaurants and shops, so different from New Zealand. Nigel and Olga choose their food from a glass cabinet. Nigel pays and they both go and sit at a table for two people. I am staggered. Now I have to pay for my own meal as well. I choose the cheapest possible meal and sit on a high stool a little away from them. Neither of them look at me as they lean close to each other and talk in hushed tones.

After I've finished my meal I go over to them and say, 'I'm feeling tired. I think I'll go back to our room.'

Nigel looks up at me and smiles. 'Right you are,' he says.

Olga acts if I'm not there.

Back in the room I have a shower, get into bed and watch *Singing in the Rain* on the television. It's strange hearing it all in German. I keep telling myself that Olga, not being that young, is probably not feeling well, that she will be better tomorrow.

When I hear them opening the door I switch off the television, push myself down under the covers and pretend to be asleep.

They come into the room.

'Thank God, she's asleep,' Olga says.

'Shhh,' Nigel says.

The next morning I stay in bed until they've both had their showers. While Olga is in the shower Nigel takes some clothes out

Olga

of her case. 'I think we should only take enough clothes to put in our backpacks,' he says to me. 'We can leave the rest here.'

'Right,' I say. 'Where will we leave them?'

'They said we could leave them in the office downstairs because we'll be staying here when we get back.'

'Right,' I say.

Olga comes out of the bathroom. She still doesn't look at me but smiles at him.

I go into the shower and put my face up to the needles of water. I feel sick with worry. I must talk to Olga and remind her that she was going to pay for everything, that I haven't enough money. Surely, I think, she must realise that.

I follow them as they walk, arm in arm. We go into ancient stone churches and look around. Nigel smiles at me sometimes, so that is something. Olga, if she happens to turn in my direction, looks at me with what seems like hatred. Her eyes are cold and deadly. A woman with a child in a pushchair comes into the church and asks the priest for money. He waves her outside, which really shocks me.

In the pension in Heidelberg there is a strange shower box right in the room so that we can all see each other when we undress and then have a shower. I avert my eyes when Nigel and Olga have their showers and I presume they do the same with me.

I think of the film *The Student Prince* when I think of Heidelberg. It is such a pretty university town with the Neckar river running through it and a huge ruined castle up on the hill. It is like something in a fairy story.

It seems that Olga isn't feeling well so she asks Nigel – rather petulantly I think – if he will go out and get her something to eat. 'Something bland,' she says.

I am terrified he will leave me with Olga and suggest I go with him. He seems happy about that. It is lovely trotting down the hill beside Nigel to the twinkling lights of the township. I want to ask him what is wrong with Olga. Have I done something to upset her, but I can't find the words.

When we get back, after a difficult search, Nigel puts the food – finely diced chicken and rice – on to the tinfoil plate he bought and hands it to Olga.

She looks at it with an expression of disgust on her face and says, 'I don't want it.'

I am amazed at her childish behaviour, which I have never seen before – and I am amazed that Nigel seems unfazed as he takes the plate away and puts it in the rubbish bin. We have also bought food for ourselves. I have already eaten my toasted sandwich on the way back up the hill.

We look over the castle the next day and then go down to a little museum where Nigel suggests I might like to go around by myself. He says Olga is tired and he will sit with her in a café. I am pleased not to be with them but after a couple of hours I wonder if Nigel is going to come back. Maybe they have left me here and gone on the journey without me? I know this is ridiculous thinking but it is what I feel. I long to cry, to talk to someone who is sympathetic – and can speak English. I want to go home.

Eventually Nigel does return. Alone. Olga is back in our room. He doesn't explain anything, and I don't ask.

We go on on a bus tour through wealthy suburbs the day we get to Zurich. We are not staying the night but travelling on to Munich. I sit next to a loud American man, while Nigel and Olga sit several seats back on the other side of the bus, cuddled up together. I want to tell this man how terrible I feel. I want to ask if I can leave *them* and travel with him. So stupid and impossible.

We are to stay in Munich for four days. We have a room with three beds, all in a row. Nigel sleeps in the middle and Olga sleeps by the window. I am beside myself with worry about my money situation. I just won't have enough to last me out. I pray. I talk to little sparrows, who I feel are my friends.

Olga

The first day we walk around Munich, down narrow streets, and into a big square where many people mill about, me trailing behind. I will have this picture in my head always. Nigel in his blue and white cap and blue jacket, Olga in her pink padded jacket and red hat. Always ahead of me. Sometimes Nigel gets Olga to stand in front of a statue, or particularly interesting old building, and takes her photograph, and then she takes one of him. I think of saying (but dare not), when you get home and show people these photographs, they'll never know there was someone else with you.

'Now tomorrow,' Nigel says. 'I've booked us on a tour. We'll be going by bus to those wonderful castles, Neuschwanstein and Linderhof. I see that King Ludwig lived in them. It says he mysteriously drowned.'

'Is that so?' Olga smiles at him as he goes on talking about what we're going to do.

I feel I can't breathe. This will take my last lot of money. I think of saying I won't come because I have almost decided to find a travel agent, fling myself at their feet and beg them to help me back to New Zealand. I know I will have to pay more money if I change the ticket and I'm terrified I won't have enough. Then I think, that no matter what happens, I can't let this opportunity pass by. I'll never have the chance to see these places again.

We stop in Oberammergau on the way. That's where they have the passion plays every year. We walk around the picturesque little town that has paintings of religious scenes on the outside walls of many of the houses. As usual Olga and Nigel walk ahead, arm in arm, talking quietly to each other. When we meet the others back at the bus it turns out we are going to lunch at a nearby restaurant. It will cost money that I now do not have so I tell Olga and Nigel that I am going for a walk and will meet them back at the bus in an hour. They both nod and Olga gives me a weak smile. She must know the reason I am not having lunch but it doesn't seem to bother her. I can't get over her cruelty. Because now I think, she is very cruel.

I sit on a bench outside a house that is obviously a dentist's surgery because I see the dentist working on someone's teeth. I take out the bread roll, cube of butter, cheese, and a piece of ham I stole from breakfast – the three of us do that so I don't feel guilty. I break the bread roll open and attempt to butter it with the handle of my comb, which isn't easy. Wealthy looking people in fur coats walk by. They stare at me, as if I'm the lowest of the low. Then I hear a rapping on the window behind me. I turn. The dentist is there waving me away. I stagger off, clutching my lunch to me. Around the corner is a street that leads to a bridge, over what must have been a stream, but is now ice and snow. I sit on a bench and finish my lunch, throwing crumbs to my friends, the sparrows, telling them how lost and lonely I feel. I'd always thought I was a confident, happy person. I had no idea I could feel so fragile and afraid.

I stand on the bridge and watch a ginger cat stepping knee deep (if it had knees) through the snow.

*

When we've been all over the castles, which so impresses me with their grandeur we go outside and decide to look at Neuschwanstein from a bridge over a ravine. Olga decides it is too steep and slippery for her so Nigel suggests she wait on a seat while he and I have a look. It won't take long.

We have to link arms as we slip and slide through the snow. We laugh and laugh, and for a short time I am happy. On the way back to Olga I ask Nigel if I can borrow 500 marks from him. I explain that I no longer have any money left and I don't have a credit card. He hesitates and then says, yes, he will give it to me when we get back to the hotel. I am so relieved. My life has been saved. I ask him not to tell Olga. He says he won't.

Olga 25

When Olga sees us coming towards her, arm in arm, she looks furious. I am stunned and think, my god, she is jealous. I can't believe she is jealous.

She takes Nigel's arm, roughly, and pulls him down the path.

On the bus I hear her say, 'Do you think you'll get that money back?'

*

The only time Olga is little bit nice to me is when we go to a beerhall and sit at a table drinking tankards of beer and watching people dancing, singing and having a good time.

After dinner in Vienna Nigel and I go for a walk. I am surprised at how many other people are walking as well. They seem to do this a lot in Europe. Family groups out walking. Everyone looking happy. I tell Nigel how Olga had invited me on the trip and how she was going to pay. He seems to understand and says he knows how difficult she can be, that he hates her meeting his friends because she can be so awful. I ask him why he puts up with it and he says because he understands her.

On the second night in Vienna, after Olga has been particularly deadly, I lie in bed next to Nigel's bed and try to keep quiet as I shudder and sob. Nigel hears. He gets up, sits on my bed and begins massaging my head.

'Don't tell Olga, don't tell Olga,' I whisper between my crying.

Nigel says nothing. He just goes on massaging my head, and then my shoulders. It is the most intimate and beautiful experience, and I feel as if we are the only two people in the world.

In Amsterdam there are three beds in a row in our room and one in the corner. Because I take the one in the corner (to be as far away from Olga as possible), Nigel says he will put their luggage on the bed in the middle.

'No you won't,' Olga says. 'I want you by me.'

And so Nigel does as he is told.

I stay behind when Nigel and Olga are going out for a meal, which annoys Olga but Nigel says to leave me alone. When they've gone I go down to the office and book a call to my son in New Zealand. When he answers I cry and cry and can hardly tell him anything – except that I'm so miserable. I leave him concerned and not knowing what to do.

I then go out to buy a takeaway. I find a place that sells chicken and chips. It is next to a shop that has a prostitute sitting in a window trying to attract customers.

After Amsterdam and Copenhagen we travel to Berlin for the last six days before we go back to Frankfurt and then home. On the train Olga lies across the seat with her head on Nigel's lap while I write in my diary, 'the pen is mightier than the sword.'

The hotel in Berlin is the most luxurious we've stayed in and, luckily for me, has already been paid for by Olga in New Zealand. It is here that I have some respite from her because, even though we are supposed to share our room she decides to go in with Nigel.

After days of sightseeing I can come back here and be on my own. I buy a bottle of gin and some tonic water, put my feet up and talk to myself every night as if there are two of me, the confident one and the frightened one. The confident one says, 'To hell with Olga, the bloody evil bitch.'

Every night we go to the same small bar down the road and have a reasonably cheap meal. I get talking to a woman there, who can barely speak English but, with a combination of broken English and sign language she invites me to her apartment. It is great to be somewhere I can relax. Gisela talks to me through her English/German dictionary and arranges to take me to the opera. La Boheme.

She visits me in my hotel room and I give her a drink. Olga comes in to collect something she had left on that first day and it is obvious she is furious I have found a friend. She slams the door when she leaves and Gisela sits there with her mouth open in shock.

Olga

On the night of the opera Nigel goes off to meet a man he met in a gay bar. Olga will be alone for the night. I feel so afraid to talk to her in the morning but, for now I am going to enjoy myself.

In the morning, our last morning I take the opera programme and spring into the dining room downstairs where Olga is sitting alone at a table by the window. I bounce up to her with pretend joy, when my heart is really thumping in terror, and show her the programme, tell her how she would have enjoyed it.

'Hmmph,' she says. 'At least you're telling me more than Nigel did. He hasn't said anything.'

*

On the plane going home Olga is her normal self, as if all that horror has never happened. I can't believe it but talk to her in a normal way as well.

The day after I get home I send a cheque (borrowed from my mother) to Nigel.

I never speak to Olga again.

The Gift of a Son

Up the steps, two at a time. The letter, white and square, sits alone in the box. And the tightness, forgotten, yet so familiar, is there again, like a contraction, spreading, gripping.

She stands, holding the letter, seeing Richard's handwriting. Feeling the thinness of the envelope, its sharp edges. Then she pushes it into the waistband of her jeans and walks slowly down, step by step, into the house.

*

In Katy's room she puts away ironed clothes. Crouches to collect books, jigsaw, Katy's favourite doll and the letter pokes hard into her ribs. She takes it out, folds it around the doll and cuddles it to her like a baby ...

She remembers letting herself feel everything, even the bumps under the wheels of the old Morris 8. And her heart seems to expand with excitement when another spasm spreads and tightens, tightens and goes away. She looks at him staring ahead at the road, his features dark against the window of bright sparkling day. Poor thing, it's hard on him. He doesn't know what's happening ...

*

Richard is four. He is at the table. Head down. Drawing with great concentration. If he only he was like this all the time. Quiet, good. Instead of trying to annoy her. Sometimes he's so cruel and calculating he doesn't seem like a child at all.

The Gift of a Son

'Richard.' She feels overwhelmed with love. Dear little kid, I must be nicer to him. 'Richard.' Her hand reaches out and almost scruffles his hair. And she can see, just by the slightest stiffening, that he has heard, but he pretends to go on drawing.

Richard!'

No answer.

'You little bugger. Richard...'

*

...Disinfectant smell, squeaky floors.

'How far apart are the pains?' the nurse asks. Efficient, stiff, crackling white. She looks at the mask eyes and tries to break through to the real eyes but the mask eyes turn away, cold, controlled.

'About three minutes, aren't they?' He looks at her, his eyes afraid, uncertain, wanting to get away.

'Yes. Oh I can feel one now.' She holds her stomach, presses the hardness.

'That's nothing,' the nurse says. 'You've got a long way to go yet.'

Oh no, surely not.

'You go.' The nurse says to him. 'We'll call you when it's all over.'

His relief is obvious. He brushes a kiss past her cheek and is off down the shiny corridor. Oh well, there was nothing really important to say. Except, remember to feed the dog...

In the white bed she stares at the ceiling and listens to clanking sounds and fast moving footsteps. The pains. That's what they call them but they're not really pains. Just strong gripping feelings that make her stomach go hard like a football. Maybe the baby is starting to come out? Maybe that's what they're doing, these pains? Tightening and pushing. Down and out. Her mother had her in half an hour, start to finish, nothing to it, she said.

The sister comes in. 'How are we feeling?'

'I think, maybe, it's coming out.'

The sister pulls back the bedclothes, rolls her over and pushes a gloved finger up her anus. That hurts worse than the pain. What a thing to do.

'Nowhere near it, dear,' the sister says. She is small and dark and has an Irish accent. Oh God, when will it happen?

*

Faces look down at her. The Irish one hisses in her ear. She feels it begin again. 'I can't bear it.' They put the mask to her face and she grips, holds it on, and breathes and breathes...

'A boy, Mrs Loveridge,' the doctor says. 'Bit small, he'll need special care for a while.'

She can't believe it. Is it all over? She looks down at the funny rat-like thing in the glass case. Did that come out of me? Did I have it? 'Oooh, isn't it funny?' She's never seen a small baby before, only fat pink ones. This one looks like a slimy blue rat with no chin.

*

When he finally comes, she is in the ward. She wants to kiss him, hold him, but he looks at all the other women who are knitting and reading and gives her a quick kiss on the forehead. She tries to pull him to her, make him forget them, but he moves away and her hand slides on down his arm and past his fingertips.

'Did you see it?' She feels tears pricking between her eyelashes.

'Yeah,' he says. 'Small, isn't it?'

'It's funny,' she says, hoping he will somehow reassure her. 'Looks like a rat.'

'Not a rat,' he says. 'More like a mouse. A dear little mouse.'

The Gift of a Son

How nice of him to say that. His voice sounds soft, and loving.
After a while he goes. Can't stand hospitals, nothing to say. Not like at home where you can get about and do things. All you can do here is stare out the window, and then there's nothing to see.

*

Richard is ten. There is music all around them. Crashing, exhilirating in its loudness. She looks at the podgy, brown-skinned second son. She can imagine him playing the trumpet one day, like the man in the funny hat and the bright clothes.

And when it's over, she walks with the children (except Richard) carried away with such hopes for them. Then she sees Richard (where's he been to now?), struggling through people to get to them. He doesn't have to. He knows he can meet them outside. But he makes it and stands in front of her, blocking the way.

'I hated that,' he says. And his face shines with joy ...

*

'Is my baby all right?'
  'Of course.'
  'When can I see him?'
  'I'll ask Matron.'
Why don't they tell her? They're keeping it from her, the baby is dead. She hasn't seen it since that first time and now it's five days.

The big trolley comes along with all the babies. All the babies, except hers. Curtains are pulled round the mothers. Am I a mother? She sits uncurtained and drops tears into sections of peeled orange. Chews and chews but cannot swallow. She has to face it, get used to it. Go home with him. Just him. Put all the things away. Somewhere.

Is there a reason? A reason she will gain from in the end? Has anyone else ever felt so empty? Lonely? Nothing can make her feel better. Not even dying.

*

She tries not to cry when he comes. But it just burst out of her in great gulping sobs. 'The baby's dead. Why don't you say it?'

'What are you talking about? Here.' He takes the rolled-up newspaper from under his arm, unrolls it and, with a flourish, lays it before her on the bed. 'Look,' he leans over her shoulder and points to the birth notices. She sees their name and the words, *The Gift of a Son.*

*

'You should have been taken to see your baby days ago. You should have asked, silly girl.'

I did I did. She looks down at the scrawny little thing. It still looks like a rat ...

*

Richard is seventeen. The light behind him is so bright she can barely see his face, just a black brooding silhouette.

'Richard,' she says, 'just give me a chance to say what I mean. I don't want to say these awful things. I want to reach you ...'

'You can't even talk to your own son.' His eyes glint at her. 'Write another one of your letters, then.'

'That's not fair.' She feels desperate.

'I'm going to Paul's,' he says. 'No hassles there. See you.'

*

The Gift of a Son

The responsibility is never-ending. She can't put this one aside. Forget about it until tomorrow, or the next day. The future seems like no future. She's got this terrible, fearful burden and she can't change her mind. Scream scream. All the time. Colic the plunket nurse says get his wind up soothe him lie him on his stomach on a hotwater bottle give him dinnesfords be constant don't let other people nurse him mother is the most important at this stage beautiful baby doing well.

*

He's in bed holding the newspaper wide with his hands. Hands that had just begun to caress so slowly, gently. Like someone else. A magic person. A person in her soul who doesn't seem to exist anywhere else. And then, as always, the baby. Screaming. Red and distressed about something, but she never knows what. Never. She picks up the writhing, screaming bundle whose eyes slice through her this way and that. She gets clean napkins, checks the pins.

'Come on,' he calls. 'What're you doing?' His voice sounds impatient, annoyed. The baby goes on screaming.

'What's wrong with you?' She holds it away from her, looks at the taut stretched face that won't tell her. 'For God's sake!' She shakes it so hard it seems like a rag doll. 'What's wrong with you? What's wrong with you?' She bangs it down on the table, and hits it across the mouth.

She is horified at the sudden gasp of silence. At the face turning blue, the deepening imprint of fingers on the cheek. My God, my God, will it ever breathe again? And then it does. With an explosion of high-pitched frequency she's never heard before. She picks it up, presses the face between her breasts to muffle the noise, and to comfort.

'What the Hell's the matter?' he yells.

'I pricked him. It's all right.' *Don't come out. Don't come out.* He'd kill her if he saw the baby's face.

'For Christ's bloody sake.' She hears the paper fall to the floor and the sound of him heaving himself over and switching off the bedside light. Thank God.

She walks out to the back porch. Stands nursing and rocking herself and the baby. 'Mummy's so sorry, so sorry, Poor wee Richard.' Listening to the shuddering sobs subside and the sound of her own heart thumping.

Dear Mum and kids,

I've joined the varsity squash club, had some good games. Saw a lot of the Morgans last weekend. Mrs Morgan is great to talk to. She and I sat and talked all afternoon about politics, the nuclear issue, all sorts of things. Their oldest daughter is a bit like me. Came home from America after five years and on the second morning they had a big row. So I'm not the only one.

I don't know why I do it. I guess, as you say, I just like the reaction. I know you've had enough. You all seem so much happier and relaxed now and me coming home and causing big dramas doesn't help. It's just that I don't feel part of the family now that you've left Dad. It's a complete new life in a new house and when I come there I feel like a visitor. You're all happy and doing things and have people coming and phone calls and I just don't feel a part of it. You seem to order me around all the time.

I don't know. I do love you, Mum, but we've never got on, have we? You don't fight with the others like you do with me. I'm really trying to look at myself, Mum. I know it's wrong to stir and get you uptight. I'm starting to see these things ...

She holds the letter on her lap and watches the words slowly distort and blur with her tears.

Owen

I was flattered when he took me to bed at this party in Ponsonby. He was a famous actor who'd been in films with people like John Gielgud and Judy Dench.

He wasn't at all passionate, which was disappointing. In fact he was a rather distant lover who seemed to be observing himself as he performed. I didn't know much then, so I supposed it was all right. I was in love with the idea of being with such an important, beautiful man. I liked holding his arm and gliding in and out of cafés as if we were royalty. We always seemed to have an entourage who gathered around us whenever we sat down. Owen would expound his ideas on religion, existentialism and so forth and they'd all listen in awe. I liked that, even though I never ever felt connected to Owen. It was as if he was the centre of his world and no-one else mattered, not even me. I was just there to make him look good. It was all an act and I was only a supporting player.

Of course, when I grew up a bit, I got sick of not having a say and I moved on through all the other men I had to go through before I met John and had the kids, but I never forgot Owen. I went on and on about him to the kids, John, and all my friends. I felt proud I'd once been his girlfriend because he'd been so well known and important.

Sometimes I imagined bumping into him in the street. Him being delighted to see me and obviously still taken by my looks. I imagined him whizzing me off somewhere for coffee or a drink, introducing me to all these important people. I imagined him listening to me, being impressed with what I had to say, apologising for how he'd treated me all those years ago. I even imagined running off with him, away from my humdrum life but, then, I'd start to feel sad about the children. It was obvious Owen would never want children in tow, his own, or anyone else's.

Then he didn't seem to be around any more and I wondered what had happened to him. Perhaps he had died.

*

One day, in a café just off Queen Street, I was killing time before I had to go to my cleaning job when a beautifully cultured voice behind me boomed, 'I know I'm speaking too loudly.'

I turned because there was something about the voice that was familiar.

A derelict, disgustingly filthy man scowled at me out of a hairy, bearded face. I felt repulsed and embarrassed and was about to turn away when I recognised those wonderful eyes. 'Owen,' I ventured. 'Is... is that you?'

'Anita,' he boomed again, as if he'd only just seen me yesterday. 'Do you have a cigarette on you?'

'I don't smoke, Owen.'

'Ah well,' he flung his arms wide and looked at me intently.

A man, who was obviously his social worker, put two cups of coffee on their table and sat down.

Owen gave the man a smug look and turned to me in glee. 'We've had sex, haven't we?' he boomed, so that even a fly in the farthest corner could have heard.

'Yes, Owen,' I muttered, aware of the shocked silence around me.

'You see,' Owen said to the man. 'I used to be normal.'

The man gave me a polite smile.

'How about buying me a packet of cigarettes?' Owen gave me an appealing smile.

'Well,' I said. 'I'll give you the money and you can get them yourself.' I fished in my bag for the ten dollar note I knew I had.

'You do it,' Owen insisted. 'They won't let me in the shop downstairs.'

Owen

'Oh,' I said, wondering what he'd done but imagining the chaos he might have caused. He'd always been provocative, loved causing a sensation of some sort. I began to wonder if that had been a sign of his sickness from way back. He was always saying God had spoken to him about this and that but, at the time, we'd all thought he was putting it on.

After I'd got the cigarettes I sat beside Owen to show the social worker that I considered Owen a person worthy of respect, and was immediately overwhelmed by a stench so terrible it took all my willpower to stop myself from retching.

It turned out that Owen and the social worker were on their way to court because Owen had caused some sort of disturbance on a bus. I wanted to say to the social worker, is this fair? Surely he needs looking after? But I couldn't say it in front of Owen.

'Where are you living now, Owen?' I asked, leaning back from him so the stench wasn't as bad.

'Here and there.' Owen waved his arm in the air.

'He's living in a council flat in Newton,' the social worker said.

'By himself?' I gasped.

As the social worker nodded, Owen said, 'Don't speak about me as I'm not here. I deserve respect!'

'Sorry,' I said, as I glanced at my watch.

'We're not boring you, are we?' Owen boomed.

'No no. It's just that I have to go to work in a minute.'

'Work?' Owen put his head back as if he were still someone extremely important and looked down his elegant nose at me. 'I could be working if it wasn't for those vile creatures.'

I waited for more but Owen was now lighting a cigarette and humming to himself.

There was so much I wanted to say, so much I wanted to ask but I knew I wouldn't get a straight answer.

We left the café at the same time. I followed Owen and the social worker down the stairs. At the bottom Owen stood as if he were on a stage and expounded to the passing crowd,

> *Methought I heard a voice cry 'Sleep no more!*
> *Macbeth does murder sleep', the innocent sleep,*
> *Sleep that knits up the ravelled sleeve of care,*
> *The death of each day's life, sore labour's bath,*
> *Balm of hurt minds, great....*

And here the social worker took his arm and pulled Owen away with him along the road to the bus stop.

I stood watching, clapping my hands feebly because I had been so carried away by Owen's magnificent performance.

I sat in my car feeling numb, as I gazed up the road in the direction Owen had gone. Then I put my head on the steering wheel and cried.

Letter From America

1956

When Beverley and I step off the tram at Perrotts Corner we nearly walk into the arms of two American sailors. The blonde one says to me. 'Know any places to go around here?'

'There's not much open on Sundays,' I say, thinking how handsome he is – and how boring and dead Wellington must be for someone like him.

'We could show you around,' Beverley says.

'Thank you, ma'am.'

They tell us they're off the icebreaker, the Northwind, which is in Wellington for four days. The blonde one's name is Dan and the dark one is Ray. We tell them our names, Eleanor and Beverley, and then walk with them down Willis Street. Beverley is in front with Ray, and I am behind with Dan.

I know people are looking at us and thinking we're cheap sluts going with American sailors - but I don't care. I know for a fact that the American sailors are really nice and respectful, because we've met quite a few – Beverley, my sister, and I. None of them have ever tried anything they shouldn't with us, not like New Zealand boys. It's *so* important to be respected. George, the last sailor I met, was off the Eastwind. He and his friend Zeke (who liked my sister) came and stayed at our house and had huge political arguments with Mum and Dad. Zeke and George slept in my room and I slept in the spare bed in Marion's room. I really really liked George but I only wanted to be his friend.

I already feel different about Dan.

We go to the Rose milk bar in Lambton Quay. Dan and Ray buy icecream sundaes for Beverley and me, and milkshakes for themselves. They are *so* polite to the girl behind the counter and *so* polite to us when they put them in front of us. That *so* impresses me.

When we're walking back along Lambton Quay Dan tells me he is married. I nearly fall over with shock - and disappointment.

'How old are you?' I gasp.

'Twenty,' he says.

'Wow,' I say. 'Do people get married young in America?'

'Not everyone.' He smiles and asks me how old I am.

'Eighteen.' I imagine his wife. She'll be attractive and nice. She'll look forward to his letters.

For the next three days I spend all my time with Dan. I take him home to meet Mum and Dad. We have pressed sheep tongues for dinner and I am embarrassed when Dan can't eat them. The idea of eating sheep's tongues horrifies him so Mum cooks him a couple of poached eggs.

It is obvious Dan is shocked when he discovers Mum and Dad are Communists but he still seems to like them.

Dan borrows Dad's clothes so no-one will know he's an American sailor but, somehow, he still looks like one. He hires a car and we go for a drive around to Eastbourne, sit and look at the sunset across the harbour. I won't let myself think this won't go on forever.

I won't, I won't.

We kiss, and it is so beautiful. He doesn't even try to put his hand down there.

The next night when Beverley, Ray, Dan and I are lying on the sand on Lyall Bay Beach, Dan suddenly whispers, 'Do you think a person can love two people at the same time?'

'Oh no,' I cry.

Beverley sits up. 'What is it? What's happened?'

'Nothing,' I say. 'It's all right.' I turn to Dan and let him kiss away my tears.

I fantasize about having Dan's baby, a blonde blue eyed boy just like Dan. Then I'll have a part of Dan with me always.

Letter From America

*

On the wharf Dan gives me his graduation badge. 'Always remember me,' he says.

I cling to him and sob and feel my heart will never mend.

*

Beverley and I stand side by side, clutching each other, sobbing and waving until the Northwind is just a tiny speck.

I seriously think of committing suicide.

*

2001

Ellie has never forgotten Dan. Thought about him through all these years. Two marriages, children, grandchildren. Talked about that beautiful blonde boy, wondered what had happened to him.

Ellie is an artist, known for her bold paintings, strong opinions about politics (more left than right) and sometimes outrageous behaviour. Her most famous painting is of an elongated man in a sailor suit, white cap on his head, floating in a sea-like sky, hands stretching after him.

Beverley is in Australia, never hears from her now. Shame.

It has been a successful life - once she was free. She lives on a cliff top overlooking the wild sea. Her house is full of paintings, hers and others. She can do what she likes, with no-one to undermine her. She has the dog, two cats, goes for walks with them all and sometimes feels lonely. But only sometimes.

In those early days with the babies her life had been full of anguish and waiting. He'd had all the power. She couldn't leave, even if she'd wanted to. How could she and the children have survived? There was no social welfare.

But so much has happened since then. So many people in her life. She hasn't needed an intimate relationship with a man. More trouble than they're worth. Needy, helpless, hopeless. She's not into looking after anyone, except herself.

She has a nice life. People coming to stay. Attention when she has an exhibition. Grandchildren to have fun with.

*

Then Carol invites herself for the weekend. She's an actress who has been distraught ever since Ken (the important man) left her for another man. So humiliating. Would have been better if it was a younger woman.

Now something has changed in Carol. She looks younger, thinner, eyes bright with happiness. Secretive and longing to be asked.

They walk along the cliff top, dog running madly in circles, cats following sedately, tails straight up in the air.

'Okay, tell me,' Ellie asks. 'What's happened to make you so happy?'

'I've met someone.'

'Oh yes?'

'He's just lovely.'

'How did you meet him?' Thinking how sad that women can only feel valid when they've got a man. Still, she lets Carol rave on about his qualities, the things they do – even the details of their sex life.

'How old is he?'

'Sixty-four. But he doesn't look it. He's really looked after himself.'

'If I ever consider a man,' Ellie says. 'Not that I want one – I realise they're too young. Those of my age seem like my grandfather.'

'I know what you mean,' Carol breathes. 'I've made such a fool of myself at times, especially in the theatre world with all those younger, virile actors – the ones who aren't gay, I mean.' She runs ahead, her arms spread wide in obvious exhilaration. 'I love being here,' she yells. 'You're so lucky.'

When Ellie catches up with Carol she asks, 'How did you meet him?'

'Through a friend.'

'What friend?'

'You don't know her.'

Later, when they're sitting by the roaring fire drinking wine Carol says. 'I didn't meet him through a friend.'

'I did wonder.'

'I met him on the internet.'

'Really?'

'Everyone does it now. Didn't you know?'

'You're joking.' How sad she thinks.

'Think about it,' Carol says. 'How else can people meet people? We're too old to go to bars, or whatever.'

'But don't they lie about themselves?'

'Some of them might. One bloke turned out to be married – but most of them are okay.'

'You mean, you've done this a few times?'

'Yes. And I've met some really nice men, but David is the star. You'll have to meet him.'

'I'd love to.' Would she?

*

After Carol has gone Ellie feels as if she is in love. She plays romantic music on her stereo, imagines dancing with someone beautiful, walking with him along the beach or down through the bush. Travelling with him around the world.

Then she wonders, just wonders if she could find Dan on the internet. Type in Northwind and see what happens. Maybe he is divorced now, or his wife has died? How romantic to meet after all these years and fall in love again.

She spends days on the internet. She types in US coastguard icebreaker Northwind 1956 and finds a reunion site where she can leave a message. She asks if anyone knows Dan Baxter who, at the time, lived in Tacoma, Washington. Then she puts the date she met him and her name.

Three days later, to her surprise, a man named Paul O'Neal sends her an email. He tells her he has investigated (in fact he has obviously gone to a lot of trouble) and found a Dan Baxter in Beverly Hills, Florida. She is thrilled and sends an email back to thank him. She explains more about how she met Dan and how she'd like to know what has happened to him. He returns an email telling her he is a retired naval officer and says she sounds like a lovely person. It thrills her to have such easy contact, right here in her own room, with someone who lives across the world.

She writes a letter to Dan, a careful letter because she doesn't know his situation, or if he is the right Dan Baxter.

A week or so later, when she drives to the post office, not thinking anything, she finds a letter from America. Her insides do a somersault because she knows it is from Dan. Hopefully her Dan. She puts the letter in her bag, not wanting to open it until she is back home and seated in just the right place. How wonderful if he really were on his own now. She imagines him coming to visit. Her meeting him at the airport. Recognising him immediately. An older, slightly greyer version of him, but just as handsome. They hit it off immediately, fall into bed laughing about how long it has taken before they finally had sex. Him telling her he still thinks she is beautiful. All her friends and relations will be so taken with the story of how, after all these years, they have got together again. Such a romantic story.

Letter From America

She puts away the groceries, cats and dog crowding around, looks at the letter sitting with the bills on the table, feels her heart skipping with fear and excitement. Finally, after making a cup of tea, she sits in the sun by the big window and opens the letter. One page, hand written.

Dear Eleanor,

I believe I am the Dan Baxter you are looking for. I remember meeting you and Beverley in Wellington when our ship was docked there. I have thought of you often over the years and wondered how you were and what has happened to you. I was delighted to receive your letter, even though it took a little explaining to my wife of 45 years!

My email address is below. I hope you will email me and tell me more about yourself, and I will do the same.

Warm regards, Dan.

He is still married. She will just have to adjust her thoughts and feelings, send him a friendly email and see what happens.

*

The emails flow back and forth. She tells him about her life, children, grandchildren, how she met Ralph, the father of her children (not long after Dan), how it turned out to be an unhappy situation. And then the five years with Barton – less said about that, the better. She tells him about her art, where she lives, the bush and river, the ocean, all so close, the books she reads, films she likes...

He tells her about his family. Three girls, six grandchildren. How he and his wife, Shirley, are Baptists and very much involved in the church (this is a bit of a disappointment but she tries to push it away), the trips they've had, how long he stayed in the navy, which was years until he took a shore job – still with the navy. He tells her how he remembers her parents and confesses he was shocked they were Communists but that he found it interesting talking with them. He asks about her sister, about Beverley, informs her that Ray and his family were all killed in a car accident. That makes her feel so sad, and she wishes she could tell Beverley.

Then he sends her a photograph of himself and his wife.

She has a neat cap of short wavy hair, plain outfit, and a pearl necklace around her neck – a matronly, sensible looking woman.

He is a stout man with jowls and, oh God, nothing like the Dan she knew (if she met this man now she wouldn't look at him twice).

She buys a scanner so she can send photographs of herself and spends some time finding those that are the most flattering, so he can see she still isn't too bad. He is obviously impressed. He tells her she is still gorgeous, like the girl he knew, and she is thrilled by that and makes herself remember Dan the boy – so she can continue writing to him. It seems Shirley has trouble with her spine, some degenerative thing. Ellie tries to control her hopeful imagination.

He sends photographs of his impressive house and park-like gardens – and she sends photographs of hers. He tells her he always knew she had a special flair.

Then he sends some photographs of him when he was on the Northwind – *and she has him back. That beautiful boy.*

They discuss politics and she tries to be open-minded when he tells he is a republican and thinks George W Bush is an honourable man. He tells her that he and Shirley have been on anti-abortion marches. She is shocked, even though she isn't keen on the idea of abortion. He also tells her that he doesn't approve of homosexuality.

Then it happens. 9/11. Twin towers. Terrorists. How dare they attack the land of the free. She knows she can't say what she really thinks at such a time of crisis. But to her it is not surprising.

He is all for the invasion of Afghanistan so they can get rid of the Taliban and Osama Bin Laden who is responsible for the attack. She says there are better ways to do this than killing innocent people – women and children she emphasises – but he doesn't seem to hear. She wants to ask why he is against abortion when he thinks it is okay to kill adult human beings. She wants to suggest

Letter From America

that Osama Bin Laden was employed by the CIA, that his family at one time were friends of George W's father.

It is harder to write to him now because there isn't much to say. But she still makes the effort, talks about nice, insignificant things. Then one of the cats dies and he sends her lovely music on an email and she thinks how kind he is.

*

2003

She remembers it all getting too much when America decided to invade Iraq and he agreed with that as well. He said America was saving the world from terrorism. She talked about oil and said she thought the world was in far more danger now than it was before – and that the American government was the biggest terrorist of all.

At odd times he'd sent a funny musical card – but nothing else. She meant to answer but got side-tracked.

When a hurricane devastated Florida she thought of emailing to see if he (they) was (were) all right. But she didn't. And he didn't. And now she'll never know if he is dead or alive. But, then, the Dan she loved died a long time ago – or didn't exist at all.

Gate Crasher

People are in little groups outside the church, talking and laughing. Near the door a woman, who must be Helen, stands greeting people, taking their hands in both of hers, smiling. Some people give her a hug. She's thinner now – and older. I wonder where Saffron is. Would I recognise her? She was only five when I first saw her, five years younger than me. Now she'd be twenty-nine.

I don't want Helen to see me, even though I'm sure she wouldn't know me so I mingle with a group going inside. There's a book there for everyone to sign. Not something I intend to do. At the door a man gives me a leaflet. On the cover is Tony's photograph. I sit in a pew half way down on the left and study his picture. He looks older, different, more grey. As Mum said, his eyes looked dead – even before he died.

Soon most of the pews are filled – he must have known a lot of people in all the years he's been here.

Then the family walk past me down the aisle and sit at the front on the right, his sister Josie and husband (I still recognise them), his parents, looking pretty doddery now, Helen – and a young woman who has to be Saffron, with her boyfriend – or maybe husband? Probably husband when I see a small child holding his hand – a child of about four or five. Saffron is sobbing.

The minister gets up and says his bit. I don't know why they're having a religious funeral when Tony wasn't religious. Anyway, I hardly hear because I'm looking at the back of their heads. The family. Tony's family.

Then a man gets up and talks about Tony's life, as if it began when he came to Australia. No mention of his life in New Zealand. I just can't believe it. How can they do it? Pretend we didn't exist?

Gate Crasher 49

He was my dad. He held my hand when we went down to the beach.

Other people tell their stories about him. This man. This stranger.

Then Saffron gets up. I'm interested now, feel my heart do a little jump. She stands for awhile sobbing and then gets herself together.

'He was always there for us. Mum and me,' she says. 'He and Mum went everywhere together.' She goes on talking about this wonderful man who doesn't sound like my father at all.

I want to get up and tell them what it was like for us. I imagine marching up to the front, everyone looking at me, wondering who I am. I nearly do it, feel the energy go through me but then I let it go.

'You were a wonderful grandfather, Dad,' Saffron says to the coffin. 'I'm sorry you're not going to see Tonita grow up.'

There is a wail from the congregation and then the sound of someone sobbing uncontrollably. I look to the family and see Helen being comforted. I can't believe such a hard women can really be genuine. But there you are.

When it is all over we are invited to the house – those of us who were close to Tony. At this point I wonder if I should just go back to my brother's place, tell him what happened at this funeral he didn't know I was going to. But then I think I would have far more to tell him – and the rest of the family – if I went to the house. I'll just have to work out what I tell people when they ask how I knew Tony. Can't tell them the truth.

I decide to phone for a taxi, except I don't know the number. I ask a man standing nearby and he says, 'Are you going to the house?'

'Yes,' I say.

'Don't get a taxi, we can give you a lift, can't we, hon?'

'Of course we can,' Hon says.

They introduce themselves as Doug and Margaret and ask me how I knew Tony. I hear myself say, 'I'm a friend of his daughters.'

'Oh, you know Saffron?'

'His daughter in New Zealand.'

'Really?' Margaret says. 'I didn't realise he had another daughter.'

'Yes,' I say. 'And three sons.' And then I add. 'Saffron isn't his real daughter.'

'I'll be damned,' Doug says.

'He's got grandchildren as well,' I say. 'Five of them.'

Doug whistles and looks at Margaret. 'I'll be damned,' he says again.

*

I walk into the large beige house with Margaret and Doug, so that people will think I'm with them. There are people everywhere, in the hallway, in the huge lounge and dining-room, and some in the kitchen. Young women with black dresses and white aprons are taking food around on plates. I look around for somewhere to put my bag. I go out into the hallway again and into what looks like the main bedroom. There is huge king-sized bed in there with a few bags and things on it. There's a dressing table with a brush and comb set on it and nothing else. All very neat and boring – not like Mum's place. On the wall is their wedding photograph. It looks funny seeing Dad as he looked around about when I last saw him. There he is standing with Helen and Saffron. Helen looks very gleeful. Saffron looks shy and Tony has that dead look in his eyes, even then. When he was with Mum he was cocky and full of life. I can remember that. And I've heard all the stories about him. Mr Big who owned the major trucking company. Life of the party. Life of everywere he went.

Gate Crasher 51

When I'm in the hallway again I notice a big board on the wall covered in photographs. I take a glass of wine from a passing waitress and go over to have a look.

There are some I've seen before when Tony was a boy. It's funny seeing them here. Then I see one of him, my brothers and me, with Saffron. I can't believe it. Seeing myself, my brothers in this foreign house. It is the most uncanny thing. That was the one and only time we came over to stay. That awful time when Helen was so mean to us and Dad brought presents home for Saffron and not us – because Helen didn't want her to feel left out. Helen was such a bitch, she screamed at me, accused me of being a liar (I was only a little frightened girl missing my mum), accused my brother John of being a thief, said we were rude to her. Of course she was lying, but Dad believed her, and we were sent home early. Mum made us keep writing to him because he was still our father but he never wrote back and finally we gave up. Mum said Helen would have stopped him because she was so jealous but I thought he was a wimp and I hated him for it. How could he be so gutless as to have no contact with his children?

There are other photographs of Tony and Helen standing by a boat, a big boat – launch type thing. They remind me of those people who were on that reality TV programme years ago, Sylvania Waters, that's it. Helen's so like that awful woman. What was her name? That's right, Noeline. Noeline and Laurie. We all immediately thought of Dad and Helen – and their lifestyle – when we saw that programme.

Someone stands beside me. 'He was a lovely man, wasn't he?' she says.

'Mmm,' I say.

'How did you know him?'

'I'm a friend of his daughter in New Zealand. He had a big family there,' I say before she can say anything.

'Really?' She sounds as amazed as Doug and Margaret.

'I just happened to be in Oz when I heard he'd died,' I continue. 'So I thought I'd come to the funeral. Then I can tell Virginia and her brothers all about it – and her mother as well. She'll be interested.'

'Oh.' She looks at me out of a heavily made-up face, black around her eyes, which has run a bit – she must have been crying. 'Do you – do you know what happened to break them up?'

'He was never home, always at the pub, or playing cards somewhere.'

'I wouldn't have expected that of Tony, not the way he was so devoted to Helen.'

He wouldn't dare, I think, remembering how, as soon as Dad was with Helen in New Zealand, he never did anything by himself again, never went to the pub, or out with "the boys". Mum just couldn't believe it. Even his pub friends pointed their thumbs at the ground when they talked about the two of them. 'He must have changed a lot,' I say.

'He must have been very unhappy in those days is all I can say,' she says

'No he wasn't,' I shout. 'They were really happy. It's just that he was so selfish, and she got sick of it.'

'Oh no I can't believe that,' she says, looking towards Helen.

'Believe what you like.' I strut away, leaving her gaping after me, and take another drink from the tray the waitress is holding in front of some other people.

As soon as I walk into the lounge I see my grandparents sitting on the couch with cups of tea on their laps. Now they've lost their son and I should feel sorry for them but I don't find it easy. They glance at me without recognition. Then Saffron's little girl runs into the room, plonks herself on the couch beside my grandparents and begins talking to them. They smile and touch her, their only great granddaughter. I want to tell them about their real great grandchildren. I want to tell them that John has two daughters and he's here in Sydney, that David has a son and daughter and Kevin has one daughter and another on the way.

I turn and nearly bump into my aunt. She smiles at me and looks a little puzzled, as if she might see a resemblance somewhere – maybe I remind her of Tony, or herself when they were kids? I'd better make myself scarce.

As I pass the kitchen I see Helen sitting up at the bench by all the booze. She's holding forth like she always did, cigarette in one hand, drink in the other.

I remember our big house out on the coast, the antique furniture so different from this tasteless place. I remember sitting on Dad's knee when we were watching the kid's programmes on TV. I remember Dad out in our games room playing table tennis with the boys. I remember him and his friends playing pool there as well. I remember Mum constantly waiting for him to come home, getting really upset when he didn't. I remember when Mum said she'd had enough and Dad was so distressed he cried. I'd never seen Dad cry before. Even when he had the affair with Helen, he still wanted Mum, said he'd only gone with Helen because Mum didn't care about him anymore and Helen made him feel wanted and important.

I go outside on to the sloping lawn. There are a couple sitting on the verandah steps talking quietly, some kids are running about. I wonder who did the neat garden. It can't have been Tony. He never did the garden – or anything at home. Mum did it – gardening, painting, or whatever. And Tony paid the boys to mow the lawn.

I wander down to the neighbours fence. An elderly woman is bending in the flower garden. I am just about to go away when she sees me.

'Hello,' she says.

'Hi.'

She comes over to the fence, tipping her hat back and wiping the sweat from her face with the back of her hand. 'Lovely day, isn't it?'

'Bit hot for me. I'm from New Zealand and it's milder there.'

'Oh you're not? No, you can't be.'

'Who?'

'Well, he had a family there.'

'How do you know that? No-one else seems to.'

'He told me.' She looks at me quizzically.

'Really?' I feel tears pop into my eyes.

'You're his daughter, aren't you?'

I nearly say no, and then think, why shouldn't I tell her. 'Yes I am but no-one here knows. You won't tell?'

'Of course not. Come on in. I'll give you a cool drink.'

'Thanks.' I climb over the fence and follow her into her rose covered cottage – just like a fairy story. She leads me into the comfortable sitting-room, plump cushions on the couches, cat ornaments everywhere, flowers in vases. All so colourful and nice.

'I've got my own home-made lemonade here. He loved it.'

'Who?'

'Your father.'

'I can't imagine him drinking lemonade. I would have thought...'

'Sometimes we had a wine but he knew he had a problem with alcohol.' She smiles and hands me the tall glass. 'I'm Lizzie, by the way.'

'I'm Virginia.' I sit in the chair opposite her.

'Yes, I know you're Virginia. He was always talking about you, his lovely daughter.' She gets up and goes to the kitchen, comes back with a bowl of mixed nuts and raisins, puts them on the coffee table between us and sits down again. 'He regretted many things you know.'

'Really.' I feel rather dubious.

'I don't think he was that happy with –' She nods her head towards Helen's place.

'I hadn't got that impression.' I take a handful of nuts. 'Not from the people I've spoken to at the house.'

'He just resigned himself. They got on okay. As long as he did what she wanted.'

'Don't you like her?'

'Not much. She's what you call, common. A common, hard woman. You know she used to run her own pub?'

I nod.

'Well that explains a lot, don't you think?'

I laugh.

'Your father told me so much about you children, and your mother. He so regretted the things he did. He used to say, if only I could undo it all.'

'Why didn't he keep in contact with us then?' I feel pissed off.

'He did but none of you wrote to him. And, then, when your mother phoned, he just gave up.'

'What do you mean, my mother phoned?'

'She said he wasn't to contact any of you any more.'

'I can't believe that. She wouldn't.'

'It was a long time ago.' She sips her drink and looks at me.

'Are you saying Mum rang Dad and told him he wasn't to contact us anymore?' Dad must have made it up. What a bastard he was.

'Actually, I think it was Helen she spoke to.' And then her lips go into a round O as she – and I – click.

'It was her,' I gasp.

'Oh, my word.'

'We wrote lots of letters to Dad after we'd been to stay and we never got *one* back. That's why we finally gave up. We thought he didn't want anything to do with us. We just never heard from him, no presents, no nothing.'

'She intercepted your letters. That is criminal!'

'She's such a bitch.' I jump up. 'I'm going over there right now to have it out with her.'

'No!'

I turn and look down at Lizzie.

'Think about it,' she says. 'No-one will believe you and you'll look bad.' Lizzie has tears in her eyes.

'She ruined our relationship with our father. She took him away from us,' I yell.

'Just sit down. You need to calm yourself.'

I sit on the edge of the couch, wanting to leap up again and rush next-door.

'I'm sure your father died of a broken heart,' Lizzie says quietly.

'Why was he such a gutless wonder? Why didn't he come and see us, have it out with us? If he thought we'd cut him off?'

'He felt too guilty. He knew he hadn't been a good enough father, or husband.'

'I just can't believe this,' I say.

'It's true.'

'I mean everything, this, me being here. It's like a dream – or I should say, nightmare.'

Lizzie leans over and touches my arm. 'I think it's a good thing. You know the truth now.'

'What good does that do?' I still want to rush next door and kill Helen.

'The truth makes a huge difference. You'll see. Always better to know the truth.'

*

Back in the house I hear Englebert Humperdink singing the song Ten Guitars. It's really loud. *Beneath the stars my ten guitars will play a song for you.* It was one of Dad's favourites. I remember how Bill, the Maori man next door, used to play his guitar and sing this song at parties, all of us singing with him. Those were the good days.

I stand in the doorway and see Helen weaving drunkenly by the stereo as she sings, *And if you're with the one you love then this is what you do. Dance, dance, dance to my ten guitars,* - everyone sings with her - *And very soon you know just where you are...* She nearly falls over as she twirls in the centre of the room.

My grandparents smile and laugh as they watch her. They don't even seem bothered by the disgusting sight.

After pouring myself a glass of wine in the kitchen (the maids don't seem to be around any more) I decide to push myself in the gap between my grandparents on the couch.

'Mind if I sit here?'

'Oh,' my grandmother seems a little taken-aback but moves to let me in.

'This was my father's favourite song,' I say.

'Really?' My grandmother says, obviously put out because I've shoved myself between them so rudely.

'Was?' my grandfather asks.

'Yes, he died. My father died.' To my surprise I begin to cry.

'Oh dear, I'm so sorry.' My grandmother warms up and pats my hand. 'I suppose all sorts of memories have risen since – ' She glances around the room. 'Being here? In this environment?'

'Yes,' I sob.

'I know how you feel,' my grandmother says. 'We're just devastated about Tony. You know he was our son?'

'Yes.' I dab under my eyes with a tissue. 'I'm sorry.'

'Thank you, dear.'

'Are you a friend of Saffrons?' my grandfather asks.

I hesitate, wondering if I should say, yes, but then they'd know Saffron doesn't know me if she comes into the room. 'No. I know Helen,' I say. 'Though I haven't seen her for a very long time.'

'It was nice of you to come.'

'I had to.' The tears start again.

'When did your father die, dear?' my grandmother asks.

'Recently.'

'Oh dear. It's surprising you went out of your way to come to this funeral after what you've been through?' She sounds puzzled.

'I just had to.' I want to ask her so much. 'Tell me about your son,' I say.

'Didn't you know him?'

'As I said, I haven't seen Helen, or him, for ages.'

'He was a good son.' Tears well in her eyes.

I feel my heart jitter as I ask, 'Didn't he have a family in New Zealand?'

It is as if an electric shock goes through her. 'Yes he did. But we don't like to think of them now.'

'Why not?' I try to remain calm.

'They weren't very nice.' She glances at my grandfather.

'What did they do?' I try to sound neutral.

'It was the mother. She turned the children against him.' Her voice breaks.

'Are you sure about that?' I hear a quiver in my voice.

'Of course. After the children had been over here she phoned Tony and said he wasn't to contact any of them any more. It broke his heart.'

'Are you sure it was Tony she spoke to?' I so want to tell her the truth but I'm afraid of her reaction.

'He told me about it, he was so upset.'

'But... did he... maybe... it was...' I look towards drunken Helen. 'Well. How do you know you can trust her? She could have been lying to you. She could have made it up about the mother ringing.'

'Of course we can trust her. What on earth do you mean?' My grandfather is angry.

'It's just that there are things I know about her.'

'I thought you were her friend?' My grandmother leans away from me, against my grandfather.

'I didn't say I was her friend. I just said I knew her from a long time ago. Listen, why don't you ask Lizzie next door about my – about Tony? You'll be surprised at what she has to say.'

'Who *are* you?' my grandmother asks.

'No-one, I'm no-one.' I get up and walk away, leaving them staring after me with their mouths open.

In the bedroom I grab my bag and swing out into the hallway again ready to get out of this hell-hole. Then I see the board of photographs up on the wall. No-one around.

I get a pen, a red one as it happens, out of my bag and go up to the photo of Dad, us and Saffron. I draw a heart around my dad, my brothers and me, and a big cross over Saffron. Hard, several times. Then I get an old envelope out of my bag and print on it in big letters, *I FORGIVE YOU DAD. LOVE, VIRGINIA.* I slip it under the photograph with the message showing, throw the pen back in my bag and rush out the front door, banging it as hard as I can behind me.

Waiting For Jim

You stand, heels digging into the shag-pile and stare at the door. You would recognise the gouges, scratches, fingerprints ten years from now. You look along the skirting board for other familiar things. You wonder if you could write them down from memory. Then you realise you've forgotten. It can be done. How amazing.

*

Jim has closed the front door and is swaying and bumping down the hallway. You take a breath and move back. Loosen fists to hands. Let them go. Limp limp ...

He peeps round the door. 'Sorry–I'm–late. Something–came–up ...' He enunciates every word with care.

'Don't worry. They're not having dinner till eight.'

There is a silence while he stands there. Staring.

You begin to feel more confident. 'I've put the sauna on for you. Thought it might relax you. After such a long day ...'

'Oh ... Thanks, love,' he says, as if he can't quite believe it.

'Come and sit down. I'll get you a drink.' You feel the swish of your skirt against your thigh as you walk to the drink cabinet. Not often you wear decent clothes, going-out clothes. You remember that time when you were a schoolgirl in uniform going home on the tram. Later, by coincidence, you caught the same tram back to town but this time dressed in good clothes, going-to-town-on-a-Friday-night-clothes. Feeling as different from that irresponsible schoolgirl as could be. *And* the conductor didn't recognise you. Funny how you've never forgotten that occasion.

'Ice?' You open the already prepared ice-bucket

Waiting for Jim

'What's all this for?' he asks, taking the glass when you hand it to him.

'Well, as I said,' you turn to pour yourself a gin and tonic (and so he won't see the insincerity in your face), 'you've had a long, hard day ... Not everyone has to work such long hours as you ...' Watch the sarcasm – it'll be the downfall of you. You swing around and smile and sit in the chair beside him. 'We're going out to dinner. Nice to have a drink before we go. Relaxing ... do you like my new skirt?'

'Yeah ... Yeah ...' He sips at his drink. Well, it's hard not to in this environment with a nice tall crystal glass in his hand. He does it well. Good at shaking the glass so that the ice clinks against the sides. A pretty sound. You don't mind it.

There is a long silence and then he says, 'Where're the kids?'

You clench your fists and stare at him for a moment. Why does he never listen? 'I told you.' And that little voice inside you says, keep calm, don't do anything wrong now, it's going to be all right. 'They're at Mum's.'

'Oh yeah ...'

'How was work?'

'Think we've got that contract sewn up with old Withers.'

'Have you noticed the flowers? They're out of our garden.'

He looks up, feigning interest. 'Great.'

How nice he is. How polite. You should do this all the time. It would save so much trouble. If you were nice to him. All the time. When he came home with his excuses and lies. To think that you could have ever been afraid, felt that steel band tighten around your chest. Why don't you be nice? Go along with him. It seems so easy – as long as you keep the anger down. Way down. Further down. Till it almost comes out of your feet ...

You stretch out your leg and look at your elegant nyloned foot in the pointed high-heeled shoes. You should have been like this so long a go. You've known. Who cares about him? Why let him affect you? Spoil your life? You can run your own life. Completely.

You look across at him and see he has finished his drink. You jump to your feet, swoop the glass out of his hand. 'Have another.'

'Thanks, love.'

He'll be nicely done.

You help him strip off his clothes. Arms behind his ears like a child. Go in with him, pour more oil on the hot rocks. He sits there staring into space, towel wrapped around him to soak up all the juices ...

You close the door and stand there for a moment. This is the bit where you have to think of the children and yourself. No more tension and fear. That's all there is about it. You reach up and push the bolt (the bolt that he put up to keep the children out, what a laugh) into the socket and walk into the bedroom.

There's your face in the big round mirrow. Does it look the same, or does it have a wide-eyes look of fear? You practise smiles ... Hello, Leonie, hope I'm not late ...

*

'Hello, Leonie, hope I'm not late.'

'Joanna, of course not. Where's Jim?'

'Oh-ah. He was late home so I decided to come ahead of him.'

'Good on you.'

'Actually he was a bit – '

'You mean he'd had a few too many?'

'More than a few.' You walk with Leonie down the hallway.

'Oh Joanna. I'm so sorry.'

'I'm used to it.'

'Still,' Leonie says, going ahead into the bedroom and showing you the white bedspread covered with coats. 'It must be very upsetting for you.'

You take off your coat and lay it with the others. Then take a comb out of your bag and do your hair, studying your face in the miror, and Leonie behind you.

Waiting for Jim

'You look lovely,' Leonie says.

'Oh – I bought this ages ago.' You smile at her twisted mirror face.

Leonie suddenly rushes to you and crushes you to her perfumed breasts. 'I know how you feel. My first husband was an alcoholic.'

'Really? I didn't know you'd been married before.'

'For seven years. The children aren't Ralph's, you know.'

'Oh, I had no idea. He's very good with them.'

'He's wonderful. So there's hope for you yet.'

You decide not to say anything. You put your comb back in your bag and smile.

'Come and have a drink and meet the others,' Leonie says.

*

They stand and sit in various parts of the big room. You feel suddenly afraid and can't think of a thing to say to anyone. You keep your eyes on Leonie's back as she walks up to Ralph and tells him to give you a drink.

'What'll you have, Joanna?' Ralph asks.

'A gin and tonic, thanks.' He is such a nice sensible man. Good-looking too. If only Jim was like that. But then, you don't have to worry about Jim anymore. Can you believe it?

'Where's that husband of yours?' Ralph hands you your drink.

'I came ahead. He should be here soon.' You turn to the room, look for a corner to stand in. Until you've got your bearings and feel you can talk to someone. You know that in a minute, as soon as she sees you are alone, Leonie will come and introduce you to people. You would like to be invisible so you can watch them, listen to them. People are so interesting. You look at the art work on the walls. Good prints, nothing original. Jim has lots of originals because they make money. Good one at making money.

There are flowers on the sideboard. Freshly picked today, do you think? Or would she have bought them? You turn to the window and look at the garden. There are shrubs there but no flowers that you can see. Of course there could be some in the back garden. Should you go through to the kitchen, look through the window or go to the back door and see? Before it gets dark? Can you leave the room without attracting attention?

'Come and meet some people.' Leonie holds out her hand. Are you supposed to take it? You smile and don't lift your hand to hers.

'Monica, this is Joanna Barton, we're both on the Board of Trustees of our school. Her husband's in real estate. In fact he runs the place.'

That's something they'll have to stop saying.

'Oh really?' She looks impressed. 'What firm is that?'

'Bartons. What does your husband do?' May as well say that. After all women are only what their husbands are. See how she likes it. See how they all like it.

'He's a teacher. That's him over there.'

'My husband should be along soon,' you say as if you're nothing without him. 'He had to work late.'

'I s'pose he'd be quite busy in a job like that?'

Is she being nice? 'He's late home every night.'

'Oh well,' she laughs. 'At least I don't have that complaint.'

What complaint do you have, you wonder.

'Excuse me,' Leonie calls. 'Would you like to come through now?'

*

There are little cards on the table with everyone's name on. You are to sit next to an older man with white hair, and on the other side an empty chair.

'I hope you don't mind us starting before Jim gets here?' Leonie says.

'No, no, that's okay. Shall I ring him? Maybe he's fallen asleep?'

'I will,' Leonie says. 'You stay there.'

'Who's s'posed to be sitting here?' a girl across the chair asks.

'My husband. He had to work late.'

'What a shame. He's missing a lovely meal.'

'Yes.'

Leonie comes back. 'He must be on his way. There was no answer.'

'Oh that's good,' you say, and almost believe he's coming.

*

You concentrate on your fish cocktail so no-one will talk to you and have a little inside talk with yourself. You are feeling quite calm, quite together. And you don't regret a thing. It'll take time before you can get used to social occasions like this. They were your thing, so there's no reason why they can't be again. Once there's only yourself to think about. Don't have to worry about him. For instance if he was here now what would he do? You lift up your eyes and look around the table. He'd be holding forth so that no-one else could get a word in. Probably put his hand on the knee of the girl next to him. Begin to spill his drink as the evening wears on and then start to put you down. Jokes, jokes. Terrible jokes that no-one thinks are funny, except him. Nothing will stop him. No matter what you say. Even when you get quite clever and throw them back at him.

'Hey,' Ralph calls across the table. 'About time your old man was here.'

'I think he's on his way.'

'He's taking quite a while,' Leonie says. 'Shall I ring again?'

'It's all right. I will.' You push back your chair and walk out of the room.

In the hallway with the door closed it is reasonably quiet. You lift the receiver, dial the number and wait. And then suddenly your heart begins to beat faster. What say he does answer? But the phone goes on and on ringing.

You put the receiver down and go into the bathroom. It is still the same face in the mirror. Small and smooth. You splash a little water on, and dab it with a towel.

A Cup of Tea

My life is a mess. I'm twenty-seven years old and it's a mess. When I look at everyone else they seem so light-hearted and happy, no guilt, no anguish. If only I could go back to that. I'd be happy to be on my own, just to be free. I wouldn't ask for anything else. I honestly wouldn't.

The thing is, I can't talk to anyone, not a soul, not even Mum, especially Mum.

The train goes clicketty clack. A man on the other side of the carriage is watching me. I can see him through the black window as we zoom through a tunnel. I poke out my tongue, knowing he will only see the back of my head. Anyway, I don't want to think about him, I'm too worried. Will the amazing Miss Bourke be able to help me? What could she tell me that I don't already know? My boss, Felicity, has been to see her, said she told her some incredible things. I was quite impressed because Felicity is a lawyer and very bright, not the type to be fooled easily. So here I am on the train going to see this woman. Appointment at 2-30. I'll have plenty of time to find her place and not feel all hot and bothered. She sounds pretty witchy with all her cats, and her house is supposed to be squalid beyond belief. I thought of taking my own cup but I don't want to upset her, she might tell me something awful.

Oh well, anything is better than nothing. I can't go on as I have been. I have to find my way out of this mire, know what's going to happen. I know what I want, but what difference does that make?

As I walk through the main street, past the pub, the shops, funny little gift shop with second-hand clothes thrown in as well, art gallery across the road, I think what an interesting looking place this is. I'd never realised that before, always passed it by in a train or car. Maybe I should come and live here? But that still wouldn't solve the problem with...

...my sister. She's two years older than me. Got married young. Four kids. A hopeless dreamer at school, didn't do very well and, yet now, she's becoming really well known for her art, huge oils that I think are rather stark and uninteresting, but the critics seem to think differently, so who am I to say? She's also started writing poetry – I'd wanted to write poetry. Why can't she stick to painting and leave me to the poetry? Mum's a writer. Mills and Boon. Five of them. She also does a bit of serious writing, too. Won a competition recently. That thrilled her more than the Mills and Boon. She doesn't use her real name for the Mills and Boon. She uses the names of her grandmothers, my great grandmothers, whom I've never known. Me, I tried hard at school, did well, but what have I got to show for it? I just work in Felicity's little outfit, running around looking things up for her, didn't even finish my law degree but, because of what I did learn, I'm a real asset. Know I disappointed Mum who said, now that she's making such good money, that she'd pay for me to go back to uni. *They* think I never follow anything through. *They* don't know what it's like, the sexism, the mindless bureaucracy. I just couldn't hack it. Why should I put up with that shit? I've done all the wrong things as far as *they* are concerned, had an abortion, never had a decent relationship with a man, bummed around from here to there, but I've learnt a lot from all this experience, and one day I'm going to write about it. Then they'll see. I've always known I'd be a famous writer. Oooh I mustn't say it too loud, don't want to jinx it. It's just in my bones, the knowing.

An icy, sharp hand grips my diaphragm. Oh God, Howard. What am I going to do about Howard? How am I going to get away from him? He's gone nuts, won't take no for an answer, taking stupid risks. It's so dangerous. I don't want him to leave Natalie (my sister) and the kids. It was just a bit of a challenge in the beginning. They were both so smug in their happiness, looked

A Cup of Tea

down their noses at me, the poor loser who can't stick to anything. He was real patronising, I couldn't stand it. So, I decided to make a play for him. There was Natalie doing her own thing, him an accountant in a big firm, the name of which I am not telling you for obvious reasons. All I had to do was cry. Simple as that. One day when she had to rush off to some meeting or other I said I'd mind the kids until Howard got home. She knows I'm not a kid person but, as I told her, it's not so bad now they're a bit older. Anyway I got them a video and a pizza and left them in the lounge while I waited at the kitchen table thinking sad thoughts to bring the tears to my eyes.

Wow, it worked. He was so concerned when he came in and found me. I ended up telling him how upset I was with Natalie's attitude, how inferior she made me feel. That really got him because it turned out that was how *he* was feeling. Secretly, I thought he was just another typical, threatened man who couldn't stand his wife getting more attention than him, but it suited my purposes at the time. So, as you can imagine, one thing eventually led to another, and there we were having a full blown affair. Sexual bloody maniacs we were. I hate to admit it but I think it turned me on, the fact that I was screwing my sister's husband. And I don't think it'd been too good for them for awhile. I made him feel like he was *'the best, the best, the best...'* when it came to sex. I did things to that man that blew his mind, things that she would never have thought of in a thousand years, I'm certain of that.

I felt so powerful.

On a high.

Meeting him for lunch, going off to a motel (wonder he didn't lose his job), then going to their place for dinner at night, knowing what we'd done that afternoon, Natalie not having a bloody clue. But then, suddenly, it was all a bit much. He became like a real puppy dog and there's one thing I can't stand, men who would lay down their life for you. I want to tell them to get a grip, I want to kick and stomp on them. But shit, he'd become so besotted, really serious about leaving her! She's beginning to notice there's something wrong. She even talked to me about it, asked if I could suggest what the trouble could be. Naturally I said I had no idea but, hell, this is terrible. Not only will my sister hate me, so will my mother. My mother will hate me. I've even thought about killing him. Isn't that terrible? Sometimes I think there's no other way. If I don't he'll tell Natalie, nothing will stop him, except death. *My* life would be ruined, never mind Natalie's.

*

Miss Bourke's house is down below the road, just a tiny run-down little place. I open the gate, make my way down the uneven path and knock on the front door. Three cats appear and rub themselves against my legs. I want to tell them to skitt but she might know. The door opens and she is there, a funny little lady with a face like a shiny red apple.

'Come in, dear,' she says. 'Excuse the mess, I haven't been feeling too well lately.'

I notice the cats around her ankles and more on the table as I follow her into the house. Never have I seen anything so filthy in all my life. It is unbelievable, dried cat food and Lord knows what else on the floor and table. I have to will myself not to vomit. I put my hand to my nose, as if I'm rubbing it, try to block out the appalling odour. How can anyone put up with this?

'Sit down, while I pour the tea,' she says. 'It's all ready, you're here on time.'

'Thank you.' I watch as she pours the tea from a black stained aluminium teapot into a filthy, stained cup with something that looks like lipstick around the rim. 'Aren't you having one?' I ask.

'No dear, I've had rather a lot today.' She pushes the cup and saucer towards me.

A Cup of Tea

I look into the amber liquid and see tea leaves and other debris floating. My stomach does a lurch. 'I'm not much of a tea drinker,' I say.

'You've got to drink it, dear,' she says, as a cat jumps on the table, it's tail almost going into my tea. 'Otherwise I won't be able to read your cup.'

'Right.' I put the cup to my lips and sip, pretending I am somewhere else, at a friend's house, sitting across the table from my mother, anything.

Finally there are only the dregs left.

She takes the cup and looks into it for some time. 'Hmm.' She looks serious.

I feel as if the blood has stopped flowing through my veins. 'What is it?'

'Confusion,' she says. 'I can't seem to make anything out, just deep dark confusion, everything massed together.' She turns the cup around, slowly. 'I see. I'm not sure. It's too black.' She shakes her head. 'I can't help you,' she says, suddenly.

'But why? Surely you can?'

'I'm sorry. You must get home, make things better before it's too late.'

'Is that all?' I watch her painstakingly pull herself to her feet. 'I thought it took an hour.'

'I won't take any money from you. Just go.' She picks up a black cat and hugs it under her chin, waiting for me to collect my bag and coat.

*

I run along the beach front in a lather of sweat and fear. What on earth was Miss Bourke talking about? What home did she mean? My flat? My mother's house? Natalie's?

*

Natalie's house is silent as I open the door and creep inside. Everything is extremely tidy.

'Natalie,' I call. 'Are you here?' I wonder where the children are and then I think that maybe Natalie has taken them to their dancing, or music, or something lessons, but why has she left the door unlocked?

At that moment Natalie comes down the stairs carrying a suitcase.

'Natalie,' I say. 'Where are you going?'

'I'm off to the airport.'

'What? But why?'

She doesn't say anything as she drops her bag by the front door and goes into the kitchen.

'For goodness sake, Natalie,' I say, following her. 'You've got to tell me what's happened. Where are the children?'

'Why are you asking about them? You don't even like children.'

'I like *your* kids.'

'Well, that's good,' she says, 'because you can help Howard look after them.'

She knows, she knows. Oh my god! 'What do you mean?' I feel as if my heart has screeched to a stop.

'I'm just waiting for a taxi.' She sits at the kitchen table, looking tragically beautiful, her wavy red hair piled up on her head with tendrils curling around her ears. She is so amazingly calm. I have never seen her so calm.

'I'm really sorry Natalie.' I stand in the doorway, afraid to approach her. 'It's my fault. Don't blame Howard.'

She frowns and looks up at me. 'Don't blame Howard?'

'It was me. I led him on. It wasn't his fault. Please, you've got to believe me. I know he really loves *you*.'

She stares at me, her mouth open. 'You've been having an affair with my husband?' She rises up from the table. 'You bloody evil bitch, you've always hated me!' She is on me, pulling my hair, scratching my face.

A Cup of Tea

'I'm sorry, I'm sorry,' I scream, terrified that Natalie is going to kill me.

'What's going on?' my mother yells.

Natalie pulls away from me. We both stare at our mother, and Natalie's children, as they stand, horrified, in the doorway.

'This bitch has been having an affair with Howard,' Natalie screams.

'You must be joking,' my mother says.

'She just told me,' Natalie screams.

My mother turns and ushers the children into the lounge. When she comes back she says to Natalie. 'Your taxi's here.'

'I can't go now!' Natalie turns this way and that, her hand to her head, like a tragic opera singer.

'Yes, you can,' my mother says.'You mustn't miss this opportunity. Not for anything, or *anyone!*' She glares at me.

*

It turned out that Natalie was off to Auckland to the Montana Book Awards. Her book of poetry was on the short list. It seems I was told but 'being so selfishly into myself' I obviously couldn't remember. Anyway the book won. Of course. And, Natalie is still with Howard, who was devastated when he found out what I'd done. Whatever he'd felt for me went out the window when he realised he was about to lose Natalie forever. So now I'm on the outer. None of them want to see me, except my mother who dutifully visits me, and is also paying for me to finish my degree. I don't think my mother can bear to have a daughter she can't brag about, so it's the least I can do.

Mum and Cassandra

I'm sitting on my bed reading the Woman's Weekly when a flash of color catches my eye. There's Wendy coming down the steps to our house, and she's got her mother with her. Why is she bringing her mother? It couldn't be a worse time. I rush into the hallway and thump on the bathroom door. 'Mum, Wendy and her mother are here. Get out of the bath.'

'Is this one of your jokes?' Mum calls.

I open the door and peep in. Mum and Cassandra are leaning back at each end of the bath covered in frothy bubbles and drinking wine. 'No,' I hiss. 'Please don't let them know you've been in the bath together. Please!'

'Oh for goodness sake.' Mum finishes her wine and puts the glass on the window sill.

Cassandra raises herself out of the water. Froth slides over her breasts and down her body.

I close my eyes.

The doorbell rings.

'Oh shit,' I say.

'Wait till I get downstairs.' Cassandra grabs her glass and the wine bottle.

But it's too late. Philip is letting them in. 'I'll never forgive you,' I say, 'if they find out you've been in the bath together.' I close the door, take a deep breath and go to meet them. 'Hi, I've just been doing my homework.'

'We were going for a walk, it's such a lovely afternoon,' Wendy's mother says in her false put-on voice. 'And we thought we'd call in. I hope that's all right? Is your mother home?'

'Ah ... she's in the bath. I'll get her. Mum,' I call. 'Mrs Duncan's here. And Wendy.'

'Won't be long.' Mum calls.

How is Cassandra going to get out of the bathroom without Mrs Duncan seeing? If only our lounge and hallway wasn't all open plan.

'Come into the dining-room,' I say, pushing Wendy in that direction. 'It's more cosy in there.'

'But I want to see your lovely view.' Wendy's mother swoops across the lounge room to the big bay window. 'Isn't it just divine,' she gasps. 'We don't see anything from our little cottage. How I'd give my eye teeth to have a view like this.' She slides along one of the church pews my father bought from a church that was being pulled down, and leans her forehead against the window.

At that moment Mum, the big bath towel wrapped around her, comes out of the bathroom, closing the door behind her. 'Just got to get dressed,' she calls. 'Amanda, put the jug on, will you?' She runs down the stairs.

Philip comes out of the TV room. 'I'll do it,' he says. 'You come and help me,' he calls to my little sister, Ruth, who is lying on her stomach by the television, drawing pictures. I watch her through the glass doors as she puts down her pens and jumps up. I'd rather she stayed there because if she comes in here and sits with us who knows what she'll say? She really loves Cassandra.

'Where's that other lady?' Mrs Duncan asks, glancing at a magazine lying on the coffee table.

'Our boarder? I think she might have gone out. She goes out a lot. We hardly ever see her.' I smile at Wendy who gives me a sick sort of smile back. Then I notice the magazine Mrs Duncan was glancing at. It's called *Circle* and has a picture of two women on the cover holding hands. Did Mrs Duncan really look at it? Maybe she didn't? I want to take the magazine off the table, but I can't can't make it too obvious.

'I always say,' Mrs Duncan says, as she looks through the window again, 'that there's nothing like Wellington on a beautiful day, especially a winter's day like this. Everything's so crisp and clear. Look at those mountains. Aren't they just divine?'

'What did you get for your science test?' Wendy asks. 'I only got a B minus.'

'So did I!'

Wendy's face lights up.

'Do you know?' Mrs Duncan says. 'That Wellington harbour is supposed to be the most beautiful harbour in the world?'

'I know,' I say.

'Hello.' Mum comes up the stairs. 'I hope Amanda's been looking after you.'

'I've just been admiring this simply divine view,' Mrs Duncan says. 'You must be so happy living here.'

'We are.' As Mum sits down she takes the magazine off the table and puts it upside down on the seat beside her.

'I hope we didn't get you out of the bath too soon,' Mrs Duncan says to Mum. 'You should have told us to go away. We wouldn't have minded, would we, Wendy?'

'Nothing to worry about,' Mum says.

Philip comes in with a tray of mugs and the coffee pot. He puts them on the table. 'I've made coffee,' he says. 'Maybe you'd rather have tea?'

'No no, coffee's fine.' Mrs Duncan says.

Philip picks up the magazine and puts it on the table again. Then he sits and begins to pour the coffee into the mugs. 'Milk?' he asks Mrs Duncan.

'Black for me.' She pats her stomach.

'You're not fat,' Mum says, taking the magazine off the table and holding it on her lap.

I look towards the bathroom. It seems so silent. What is Cassandra doing in there? What say Wendy or her mother want to go to the toilet?

Ruth comes running into the room with a plate of gingernuts. She puts them on the table, climbs onto Mum's lap and puts her arm around Mum's neck. 'Where's Cassie?'

Mum and Cassandra

'I don't know.' Mum looks vague. 'I think she's gone out.' She kisses Ruth's forehead.

'Where? She was going to take me to the park when she'd finished having a bath. Why did she go without me?'

'She's probably just popped down to the shop,' Mum says. 'Have a gingernut.' She reaches toward the plate.

'Why did Cassie go without me?' Ruth pummels Mum's chest with her fists.

'Come with me,' Mum says. She takes Ruth by the hand and almost drags her out to the kitchen.

'She seems very fond of your – your boarder,' Mrs Duncan says.

'Yes.' My fingers want to get around Ruth's neck and squeeze and squeeze.

'I hope it's not too strong,' Philip puts the mug of coffee in front of Mrs Duncan.

'Thank you, darling. I wish I had a big handsome young man like you to look after me. I've only got two rebellious daughters.' She puts her arm around Wendy and pulls her towards her.

'Don't, *Mum*,' Wendy says.

Mrs Duncan gives a tinkling false laugh. 'Oh, we mothers can never do anything right. You children are just so judgmental. Really, one day you'll realise the sacrifices we've made for you.'

'I was just saying,' she says, when Mum comes back into the room, 'that we mothers can never do anything right. Children are so judgmental, aren't they?'

Mum takes a sip of coffee. 'Mmm.'

Wendy stands up. 'Excuse me,' she says to her mother. 'Can you let me past. 'I want to go to the toilet.'

'Go to the outside one,' I hear myself gasp.

Wendy looks at me in amazement. 'Why?'

'Don't be silly, Amanda,' Mum says. 'I haven't left any towels or underwear on the floor, it's all in order.' She laughs. 'She's so fussy, hates people seeing our mess.'

'Not when it comes to her bedroom.' Philip sounds puzzled.

I try to send a psychic message to him. Think Philip, think. I watch Wendy go into the bathroom and close the door.

When she finally comes out again she looks normal so I decide to go in myself. Cassandra must be hiding in the shower box, that's all I can think. But when I look she isn't there. I can't believe it. She can't have just disappeared into thin air. She must have climbed out the window. It's not that far from the ground. I feel such relief. And then I hope none of the neighbours saw her.

*

'Your house is quite high up on this side, isn't it?' Mrs Duncan presses her head against the window and peers downward. 'Oh my goodness,' she gasps. She turns to Mum, her hand to her mouth. 'I think you've got a burglar. There's someone down there.'

'What!' Mum and Philip jump up, knocking over the milk jug. Milk runs all over the tray, around the sugar bowl and plate of biscuits.

'He – no I think it's a she – she's trying to climb up on to your bottom balcony. Oh, I say, she hasn't got any clothes on!' Mrs Duncan rushes to the door of the top balcony, opens it and peers over the railing. Then she turns back to Mum, Philip and me. 'It's your boarder,' she says. 'What on earth is she doing?'

'For goodness sake,' Mum yells down to Cassandra. 'I told you to wait in the wash-house.'

'It was too bloody cold,' Cassandra yells back. 'For Christ's bloody sake, aren't you going to help me?'

'It's all right Cassie, I'm here.' Ruth appears on the bottom balcony and holds on to Cassandra's shoulder while Cassandra levers herself over the railing. She thumps on to the deck and stands there, not even trying to hide herself. She just stands there looking up at us. 'This is fucking ridiculous,' she says, taking Ruth's hand and walking into the house.

'Well,' Mrs Duncan says. 'I think we'd better go and leave you to it. Thank you so much for the coffee, Philip. Come along, Wendy.'

'I don't want to come yet,' Wendy says. 'I'll see you later.'
'Please yourself.' Mrs Duncan looks at Mum. 'It's been um...'
Mum laughs. 'You'll have a lot to tell your friends.'
'Oh... I... ah wouldn't...'
'I certainly will.' Mum closes the door.

*

I sit and look down at the city while Wendy sits opposite me not saying anything. I know she'll tell all the kids at school. There have been so many times when I've wanted to leap off that balcony and sail over the city like Peter Pan. Now I just want to jump off it and smash myself to pieces so it really hurts and I die a terrible agonising death.

'I'm sorry, Amanda,' Mum says, as she goes downstairs to see Cass.

'Everyone at school knows,' Wendy whispers. 'We've always known but we couldn't say anything because you didn't.'

'What?'

'No-one cares. Honestly, Man. They all like your mum, and Cassandra. Your birthday was the best anyone's been to. We thought Cassandra was terrific. She's such fun and she seems so young and with it, so does your mother.' She begins to cry.

'What's the matter? Wendy, what are you crying about?'

'My mother deliberately came here to catch your mother out. She had a bet with one of her friends. I hate her, I hate her, I wish I could live with you.'

Jesus in the Shed

There was something different about this day, as if something amazing was going to happen. Monica had never felt so certain about anything before, and yet another little part of her told her she was being ridiculous. Still, why not believe it, the anticipation would give the day a lift.

Luke could obviously see there was something up and for an awful moment she thought he might not go to work. It took all her resources to reassure him that she had nothing planned, except the washing and the housework.

He wasn't entirely convinced and scowled at her suspiciously as he picked up his lunch-box and followed the boys out of the house. 'I might pop home later,' he muttered.

'That would be lovely, dear.'

Monica put on loose trousers and one of Luke's sweat shirts and set off for her little run, tripping along on her toes, arms bent at the elbows and held out sideways, as if she was uncertain of the world, uncertain of herself, afraid to catch the ball that had been thrown to her. Not knowing if she wanted to catch it – or would be allowed to.

Seagulls, circling and screeching, swooped down to the shiny water. Cold as it was, Monica felt as if she could walk into that mercury sea, let it slip around her, carry her where it might. She almost went down onto the beach but something told her this wasn't it. She must go home. It would happen there. So, at the bathing sheds, she turned and jogged back to the house, snibbing the door after her when she went inside, so Luke, if he did come, wouldn't be able to unlock it.

After her shower she wrapped a bath towel around her and sat at the dressing-table, feeling daring as she applied smooth beige make-up, then blusher, lipstick, did her eyebrows and lashes, piled

Jesus in the Shed

up her pepper and salt hair like they did on the soaps, tendrils floating down. Who would recognise her as the pale nothing who hardly said a word, afraid to receive his wrath, not allowed to challenge him. Sixty-one she was, just a silly old fool, too late to do anything now. Why did she still hope? So far God had done nothing for her, even though she'd been praying to him for years as she lay staring at the white ceiling.

Yesterday, just yesterday, when she'd gone for her little run she'd looked up at the blue sky, thought of the blue-eyed baby girl and realised that the little stillborn girl was her guardian angel. Of course. Little Angela, that was what she'd secretly called her for all these years. Hadn't mattered to him. He'd never wanted to name a dead child. 'Meant to be, woman, just get on with your life.' Her little girl had always been here to protect her and she hadn't realised it until now. The child had chosen not to live, knowing what would happen if she did. In the bedroom Luke liked Monica to be a little girl, dress in little girl clothes. What would have happened if he'd had a real little girl?

She envied the women who had careers, lawyers, doctors, company directors. They controlled their own lives, rushed home to modern, clean kitchens, doing everything in an important rush. As far as she could see that would never happen for her. She felt trapped, had lost her determination.

But now there was hope. Why did she feel this so strongly?

Plastic flowers in vases, Jesus on the walls. What hypocrisy when he didn't practise what he preached. It seemed to her that anything she wanted wasn't allowed, just for the sake of it. Luke would make any excuse not to please her. She should say the opposite to what she wanted, that would fool him.

She sat for some time on the back porch, revelling in the warmth of the sun, drinking the forbidden coffee, listening to her tiny secret radio, letting God and the birds see her made-up face. Then the house called her, and she knew she had to go in. 'But not forever,' she heard a light voice whisper.

As she trailed through the untidy lounge strewn with their shoes, socks, saucers of half eaten peanuts and chippie packets, she looked up at Jesus over the fire place. Huge, pale misery on the cross. Dominating the whole lounge with dark heaviness, as if he were judging her, blaming *her*. 'I'm not taking any notice of you,' she said.

Before the end of the day she would have to tidy the mess away. Now she had the day to herself and after she had washed the dishes, shoved their stiff jeans into the washing machine and hung them out to dry she would reward herself with the lunch time soaps on her secret portable television. And wait.

First she had to get dressed, get back her other face. If Luke did come home he'd thrash her if he saw her wearing the 'devil's make-up', accuse her, as always, of trying to tempt men (where on earth would she find these men, and would they want *her* if she did?). She opened the jar of cold cream, dipped a tissue in and swiped it down her cheek leaving a pale strip of road. She looked at it for awhile and then wiped around and across until all the colour was gone and she was left with a blank pudding face. She took the pins out of her hair, let it fall down past her shoulders again and packed everything into the box at the back of her underwear drawer. Then she dropped the towel, put on her bra and panties, slipped the floral dress she hated over her head, wound her hair into a tight knot, put on her cardigan, socks and slippers, and went out to the kitchen.

*

It took Monica a few moments to realise that someone was bashing on her front door. It must be Luke! She rushed to turn off the television set, grabbed it and took it into the bedroom, pushed it into the back of the wardrobe behind her sewing machine. As she ran through the lounge she glanced around to see if everything was as it should be.

Jesus in the Shed

When she unlocked the door she was surprised to see the young man Luke had just taken on as a carpenter. Bruce, that was his name.

'Hello, Bruce,' she said. 'What can I do for you?'

'I... Oh hell, I don't know how to tell you this.'

'What is it Bruce?' she asked kindly, trying to reassure him.

'It's Luke, he's had an accident, the scaffolding, it collapsed.'

'Oh dear.' She looked at his distraught face.

'He's dead Mrs Armstrong.'

Music filled the house, heavenly music played by angels in white robes, harps, horns, a huge organ. Monica beamed and looked at Bruce, surprised that he was unaware of what was going on.

'I'm so sorry,' he whispered.

'Come in and have a cup of tea. It looks like you need one.'

'I rushed over here straight away,' he said, following her inside.

'So good of you.' She went into the kitchen and put on the jug. 'Sit down Bruce. Would you like a piece of cake? I think there's still some left. That is if Luke and the boys haven't eaten it all.' She laughed, as she opened the tin. 'You're in luck. One piece left.'

'No thanks, Mrs Armstrong, I don't think I could eat it.'

She stared at him. 'No, I don't suppose you could. Did you see it happen?'

'No, I just heard him yell.' He looked at her, his eyes wide. 'I couldn't believe it when I saw him lying there.'

The music rose up again. Monica could see her blue-eyed daughter smiling and winking as she plucked at her harp. She poured hot water over the tea leaves, put the lid on the pot and turned it three times one way and then the other. 'Of course you couldn't,' she said, as the music faded.

'I think he died straight away, Mrs Armstrong, I'm sure he didn't feel any pain.'

'That's the main thing,' Monica said.

'Is there anything I can do for you, Mrs Armstrong? Matthew, Mark and John? Could I get in touch with them for you?'

'Don't you worry yourself. I'll tell them when they come home.'

'But... don't you think you should tell them straight away?'

'Why worry them unnecessarily? There's nothing they can do.'

'Right... ' His voice trailed off.

She poured the tea and pushed his mug across the table. 'Have some sugar in it. You need it.'

'Thanks,' he said, stirring in three teaspoons and biting his bottom lip.

*

It was so lovely having these kind folk, some she'd never seen before, bringing food, saying such nice things about Luke. She enjoyed the attention, felt important for the first time in her life.

And then the funeral. Monica felt like a queen as people took her hand and then passed through into the assembly hall. When it was time for her and the boys to go in, Matthew on one side, Mark on the other, and John in front, they had to push through a crowd of people around the door. Inside, every seat was taken and there were people standing around the walls. As they walked slowly to the front, the angels began playing the Wedding March. Luckily no-one else could hear it. Monica smiled and winked up at Angela. Yes, it was appropriate because she did feel like a bride as people turned to look at her. Only thing was she was wearing black instead of white, Angela would appreciate that. The long lacy gown she'd bought was lovely, and she was wearing pantihose and high heeled shoes, had piled her hair up, put on just a *little* make-up, must be sensitive to the occasion.

Luke would be so proud to hear all the wonderful things people said about him. Monica felt that he was already up there looking down, revelling in the funny stories, feeling satisfied that his life was worth something to all these people, and the boys – Matthew

Jesus in the Shed

and Mark, were in a terrible state, blubbering away on each side of her. She wondered why, considering the terrible hidings they'd had over the years. Still they didn't know anything better.

Quite a number of people came back to the house for a cup of tea, sitting in the tidy lounge full of fresh flowers, plastic ones in the rubbish tin, Jesus in the shed. She didn't feel bad about that. Only hypocrites like Luke needed to display their religion. If all these people only knew what he was really like, but it didn't matter any more, let Luke have their good thoughts, it wouldn't hurt her.

*

It surprised her that the boys thought everything was going to go on as normal, except that Luke wasn't around. She had to sit them down and tell them things had changed.

'You'll have to find homes of your own now,' she said. 'I'm selling the house.'

'What? Where are you going?' John asked.

'Won't you be lonely?' Mark looked at her as if she might be suffering from some type of mental breakdown.

'Certainly not, I'll have... I'm going to very happy. You don't have to worry about me.'

'But, well, you've never done anything for yourself. You're just a woman. You've always had Dad and us. What will you do? How will you manage?' Matthew looked at the others.

'I'll have no financial worries once I've sold the business.' She smiled at their astonished faces.

'Dad said one of *us* was to take over the business if anything happened to him.' Matthew gulped and sat down.

'I think it's better if the business is sold. You can all get jobs. I'm sure you won't have any trouble.'

'But Dad said...'

'Your father's gone. He's where he is supposed to be now.'

'But...'

'No buts, I have decided.'

'What's happened to you?' John asked.

'A miracle has happened.' Monica smiled.

They all looked at each other.

'Dad wouldn't like you wearing all that make-up, the clothes.' Matthew glared at her.

She stood up. 'You've got a couple of weeks to find somewhere else to live.'

'But you're not used to being on your own,' Mark looked anguished (it was so touching). 'You'll be lonely, I know you will.'

'No.' She shook her head. 'No, I'll never be alone again.' Not now that I have your sister, she nearly said.

But how could she tell them Angela would be with her all the time, that now the end of the day would be perfect, something to look forward to.

Inside Out

I've just thought about it. I'd rather have plump people than thin ones. That woman in her mid fifties who wants to live forever, who says she is *going* to live forever and can tell the rest of us how to do it, she looks like a skeleton. Her skin is stretched so tight over her face it seems any second it might split. In forever and ever it will be peeling off in strips and eventually nothing but bones will be left.

I suppose they'll have to stop birth if everyone lives forever...

Now where was I? That's right, I'm trying to write a story on the theme called *Writing The Body*.

*

Jessica lifts up her skirt. 'Look at my cellulite,' she screeches.

Constance stares at Jessica. Is she joking? 'Who gives a fuck?' she says.

'I'm serious. What am I going to do about it?'

'There's nothing wrong with you. You're an attractive, slim young girl, for Christ's sake.'

'The rest of me's all right. It's just the top of my legs.'

'You've got to be joking,' Constance says.

Constance watches Jessica across the table in the restaurant where they're having a meal with Constance's friend, Robert. Robert is blind and yet Jessica arranges her facial features to their best advantage. How absolutely amazing, Constance thinks, as Jessica blinks and purts and puts on this show that Robert can't see.

Or I could write about Robert and me and how relaxed I feel with him because he can't see me. I can wear my dirty dressing gown in front of him, have food on my face, sleep in my eyes. I can run around naked and not have to worry. It is so wonderful and freeing.

Robert and I talk and talk. Our minds and souls have no barrier. The outer casing cannot get in the way and distract. I think about what it must be like for him. He is judging people differently. He sees the insides.

'That friend of your daughter,' Robert says. 'She's a strange one. I didn't feel warm to her. She seems so false.'

Now I watch Jessica and Robert walk arm in arm as she leads him down to the beach. They talk and talk.

'When you've gone,' Robert says, 'Jessica's going to come over for lunch. I take back what I said about her.'

Or I could write a poem:
Souls trapped in bodies
Look out through fat and bone
I'm in here, they call
Why can't you see me?

Or I could write about Marnie who does everything perfectly, including eating like a sparrow and vomiting up when she's had a binge. When I put it to her she denies it so convincingly.

'Of course if it's true,' I say, beginning to wonder myself, now, 'you wouldn't say.'

Then there was that time in the bus when I was in Spain. All the young girls in our party considered anyone over the age of thirty as beyond interest. For the first time in my life I felt old. And angry. How dare they think of me as nothing, just because my body is older than theirs.

Even now I don't know who to fancy or consider falling in love with. I feel so young and vital but perhaps I don't look it? I feel about thirty but I'm twenty years older than that. I keep forgetting. Do I have to behave how I look? How do I look? I don't even know, really. Sometimes I catch glimpses of myself in shop windows and feel quite pleased. Other times I am shocked.

Leanora gets up at 4-45 every morning to go to the gym before work. 'If I don't watch it my body will get the better of me,' she says.

'It's already got a lot bigger over Christmas. I've got to keep it in control.'

'What do you think of this latest action of the government?' I ask.

'I never read the paper, or watch TV, don't know what's going on the world, I haven't got time for all that,' she says.

Or I could write a story about the lesbians who say it's politically incorrect to wear make-up but who secretly do. You know, they wear light brown foundation that covers all the blemishes?

I'm interested in health. I like to to keep fit. If I lived with someone who was too overweight I'd probably get annoyed with them.

Oh God.

Overseas Experience

'Keith's going to join us in Frankfurt,' Jake says. 'Isn't that great?'

'Keith from New Zealand?' Polly imagines dark red blood is draining from her body and running across the parquet floor.

'I don't know any other Keiths.' Jake frowns at her.

'But why? This is our honeymoon, Jake.'

'I thought you liked Keith.'

'I do.' She doesn't, she hates him, never wants to see him again. 'But that doesn't mean he should be with us on our honeymoon. You don't take your friend with you on your honeymoon.'

He opens the wardrobe and hangs up his jacket. 'You know how worried we've been about getting around Europe, finding the best places to stay.' He turns, smiling his bright white smile. 'He's so well travelled, knows it all.'

'I can't believe this, Jake.' As she turns away to hide her tears she sees the dentist in the window across the narrow street lead a woman into the room and help her into the dental chair. 'The only thing that's kept me going in Madrid is the thought that we'd soon be out of it. Just the *two* of us.'

'Are you depressed because you're alone every day while I do my lessons?'

'Of course not. It was a wonderful opportunity to join your language class on this tour and combine it with our honeymoon. I knew what was I was in for.'

'Oh come on, darling, we'll still have time together.' Jake puts his arms around her.

'I wanted every spare moment with you. You see so much of Keith back home. Why do you want him here?' She turns into him, presses her head against his chest, smells his tangy cologne, hears his heart beating.

Overseas Experience

'Okay, I'll ring and tell him not to come.' He pushes her away and moves to the door.

'It's too late now, you've already arranged it.' She'll only feel guilty if he tells Keith not to come now.

'That's okay. He won't mind.' He takes hold of the door handle.

'Forget it, Jake.'

'Are you sure?' He turns, his eyes hopeful.

'Don't worry, I'll get used to it.' She takes off her jacket and scarf and climbs into bed. 'I'll never understand why they turn off the electricity,' she says to change the subject. 'It's so cold.'

'We should have brought hot-water bottles.' He seems relieved to be talking about something else.

'We could cuddle up together,' she says patting the space beside her.

He laughs and gets into his own bed.

She wants to say, fuck me Jake. I need you to fuck me, but somehow she can't say it. 'It's all wrong,' she says.

'What is?'

'Well,' Polly watches the amused expression on his face. 'The hotel doesn't have enough heat but the shops have too much. It's crazy.'

'It'll be better when we get to Germany.' He reaches across and pats her leg.

She takes his hand and presses it between her thighs.

'Hey.' He pulls away and sits up. 'I must show you the itinerary Keith and I worked out.' He takes his writing pad from the bedside table. 'This seems the most efficient way to use our Eurail ticket. A day in Frankfurt, three days in Heidelberg, half a day in Zurich ...'

'Why?'

'That's how it's worked out with catching trains. We'll spend that time on a bus tour. Won't be too bad. Then four days in Munich. Keith says we've got to see King Ludwig's castles, Neuschwanstein and Linderhof. They're absolutely fantastic, he says, especially

Neuschwanstein. It's just like a fairytale castle. I think they used it in Disney films.'

'Sounds great'.

'We can go to a beer hall. Can't go to Munich and not go to a beer hall, can we? And then there's Dachau. Do you want to go there?'

'I don't know if I could face that,' she says.

'We'll see.' He turns the page. 'Two days in Vienna, four in Amsterdam, two in Copenhagen and six in Berlin. How's that? We can see the Berlin Wall, go through Checkpoint Charlie to East Berlin. Then back to Frankfurt again.'

'You and Keith have gone to a lot of trouble. It must have cost a fortune in phone calls.' She feels hurt that neither of them thought of consulting her.

'I'll worry about that later.'

'And all those letters he's written to you as well.'

'Not that many.' He pouts as he puts the list in the drawer. 'I've known Keith for a long time. We're like brothers.'

'I haven't heard from *my* sister – or brother.'

'Oh well,' he says.

She wishes they had a double bed. He is so tall it seems impossible in a single bed. When she'd suggested putting the mattresses on the floor he'd laughed and said, 'Wait until we get to Germany, I can concentrate on you then.'

She can't wait.

'By the way,' he says. 'The others thought we should try that restaurant Bill was talking about. You know, the one just off the Peurta del Sol in San Jeronimo. Really nice seafood, they say.'

'Okay, whatever you want.'

'We'll go back to the Peurta Rica tomorrow night. I know you like it.'

'It's only that I feel at home there.'

'Oh, you poor darling, I haven't been very considerate, have I?'

'Yes you have, it's all right.'

Overseas Experience

'No.' He looks thoughtful. 'I haven't. It's just that I get so one-tracked about things, you know what I'm like?'

'I expected it, Jake. You don't have to worry.'

He lies back against his pillows and puts his arms behind his head. 'So, where did you go this morning?'

'The Prado, of course. I know it inside out and back to front. I know the whole of bloody Madrid inside out and back to front. It's such a disgustingly filthy place. Everyone smokes, even in shops and the bank. I can't wait to get back to clean air and blue skies.'

'Okay, okay.' He sounds impatient, which is not like him.

'Mind you,' she pushes further down into the bed. 'I'll never regret this chance of seeing the Prado. All those amazing paintings, Goyas, Velasquez. Fancy being here at the time of the Velasquez exhibition. I've told you my favourite artist, though. Hieronymus Bosch. I think it's amazing that someone did such way-out stuff in the 16th century.'

'You've had a good time, haven't you? All those trips we've been on with the group. Toledo, Segovia, Cuenca, The Don Quixote Trail. You loved all those places?' His eyes are pleading.

'Of course I did. It's just that a month in a filthy, dirty city like Madrid is a little too much when most of the time I'm by myself. I know I'll look back later and really appreciate it, but at the moment I can't wait to get to Germany. At least it will be cleaner and more civilised.'

'I'm sorry, love. I'll make it up to you, I promise.'

*

After she's spent some time writing a letter home, telling them about the plans for the Eurail trip, not mentioning Keith, she looks at her watch. It is just after five. She glances at Jake and sees he is asleep. Oh well. She creeps out of bed, tip-toes into the bathroom and fixes her make-up. Then she puts on her jacket, hat and scarf. She'll go down to the little grocery shop on the corner, buy some cheese, ryvita biscuits and a couple of pottles of yoghurt. That'll stave off the hunger pains until they go out to eat at eight.

The father and son who own the shop have to practice their terrible English on her so it is some time before she gets back to their room. Jake isn't there. Perhaps she should have left him a note. She notices a small plastic bag on the floor. She picks it up and sees it contains a bundle of letters, Keith's of course. She is just about to put them on the bedside table when she hesitates, runs to the door and puts the chain across. Then she sits on the bed and pulls one of the letters out of the pile.

Darling Jake, I miss you so much... She freezes with shock. My god, has he been writing to some woman? Is he having an affair? Has Keith been the go-between? Does that explain... ? She turns to the last page and sees, *Love you forever, Keith.*

She folds the letter, slips it back between the others, runs to the door again and unloops the chain.

*

She is just putting cheese between two ryvita biscuits when Jake comes in.

'Hello darling,' he says. 'Did you pop down to the shop?'

'Yes, I was starving. Where have you been?'

'Thought I'd give Keith a ring and tell him you didn't mind him coming. And then I went down to the vault to put my travellers' cheques and passport away.

'You forgot that plastic bag. It was on the floor.' She watches his face as he looks towards the bed.

'Oh,' he says. 'I must have dropped it. I'd better get the key again.'

'It's nothing important, is it?' she says. 'Nothing anyone would want to steal?'

'I guess not.' He looks at her for a moment. 'Yeah, I'll take them back in the morning.' He puts the bag underneath other things in his drawer.

Overseas Experience

*

The group of six walk out of the hotel and along the narrow cobble stoned Callé Valverde, past the sex shops and prostitutes on the corner and out to the Grand Via. There are more people here than on a Saturday night in Wellington, and it is only Tuesday. Families pushing strollers and prams, people selling lottery tickets, others handing out advertising information that immediately goes on to the footpath like confetti. When they go down the steps to the Metro and across to the other side of the road she pulls her hat over her ears so she can't hear them chatting to each other in Spanish. Jake (ever considerate) turns and holds out his hand but she waves it away. They must think she is so lucky. Her friends back home envy her, she knows that. Jake, so sensitive and aware, not like the bastards they've been involved with.

*

'Hear you've decided where you're going on your Eurail ticket,' Neville says when they're seated in the restaurant. 'Sounds great.'

'Yes,' she says.

No-one says anything about Keith so perhaps Jake hasn't told them. She hopes not. She doesn't want them to know. They'd only make jokes about it and she'd feel such a fool. 'I can't wait to see some of those beautiful castles,' she says.

'And the Berlin Wall.' Jake smiles at everyone. 'We couldn't be going at a better time, could we darling?'

*

As she comes out of Customs it seems that a wave of people surge at her. She is taken over by the wave, feels as if she is drowning as she is pulled this way and that. She sees one of the children's faces. 'Mum, are you all right?'

'Yes yes,' she says.

'What a dreadful thing to happen,' someone else says. 'He was such a lovely man.'

'I just feel numb,' she says, as the trolley is taken away from her. Hands take hold of her hands.

'Is he... is he on this plane?'

'No no,' she says. 'His friend Keith came. He's been marvellous. Took care of everything. He's stayed to sort out all the official stuff about getting the body back.'

'I still can't believe it,' she says. 'There we were, so happy, standing on the swing bridge above the castle Neuschwanstein, looking down on it. Jake had been taking photographs...' She puts her hand to her mouth in an effort to control herself. 'He wanted to get one from a different angle.' She closes her eyes for a moment, breathes deeply. 'He...' A hand pats her shoulder. '... came off the bridge, stood on the edge of the ravine, and... somehow... Oh God,' she sobs. 'He missed his footing.' She can still see her hands flat on his back as she pushed, him bouncing off rocks as he rolled and crashed to the bottom. 'There was no-one else around. All the other tourists had gone to get the bus. We'd come in a rental car, you see.' She'd insisted on that – let Keith stay behind for a change. I'm sick to death of never seeing you. 'It was terrible terrible. I ran screaming through the ice and snow, slipping sliding, nearly falling, to get help from the castle.'

'It's such a tragedy,' someone says. 'He was so perfect for you.'

'I know,' she cries. 'I'll never meet someone like him again.'

'You've still got your friends and family. We're here for you.'

'Yes.' She turns into waiting arms. 'I'm so grateful. I don't know what I'd do without you.'

Wanting

That pudgy little girl and her mother. Stupid woman, giving in to her every whim. That child wanted everything. Never satisfied. 'I want white bread, only white bread.' How could the mother put up with that?

Just the two of them. Sleeping in the bed with her mother until she was five? Six? Having the mother's breast when she was quite an old little girl. What did the mother get out of that, one must ask? Was it true that the mother had a husband who was killed in the war? That child never knew the truth.

Every day she was taken to school and collected afterwards. Never allowed to walk home with her friends. The other children ridiculed her and made fun. 'Your mother's an ugly old witch. Witch, witch, ugly old witch.' How she hated the other children, wanted to go home right away to her mother who would be in the warm kitchen opening the oven and taking out hot raisin scones on a tray. 'One for you and one for me and one for you and one for me.' Spooning raspberry jam from a cut glass dish and a dollop of cream from a bowl with yellow flowers.

When they walked home from school, her mother would swing their hands between them and the other children would giggle as they ran past. She noticed but her mother didn't. Her mother's hot hand would pull her in to the little bakery just past Rongotai Terrace and they would look at the cakes and biscuits, and the pink and white meringues behind the glass and she would be able to pick what she liked. Oh, how she loved those crunchy meringues that cost two pennies for two without cream and three with cream between them. She always had the cream. Greedy, fat little girl. Then they would go up to that seat between the Hebes on Rongotai Terrace and sit there watching the planes flying down to the airport, and eat, dropping crumbs on their laps and brushing them off for the sparrows. And the children on the street below would yell and hit each other and not know that she and her mother were up there watching.

Sometimes she fantasised about her father. His name was Errol Flynn and he wrote letters to her every week. She has them still. She even looked like him with her fair hair and blue eyes. One day he was going to come and get her, take her away to America and she would live with him and have lots of friends who really wanted to know her because now she wouldn't have her mother any more, just her father. And he would take her to parties and she could do anything she liked. She wouldn't be stopped any more, wouldn't have to comfort when the fat tears rolled down her mother's fat cheeks. 'I am crying for lost love,' her mother would wail and splutter. 'Make me a cup of tea, and there's a piece of fruit cake still left in the tin.'

*

'If you lost some weight you would be really attractive,' one of the girls said to her at secondary school. 'You have lovely eyes and nice features.'

She looked at herself in the mirror and imagined herself with hollow cheeks and a thin neck. And then she thought of the apple upside down cake in her bag and didn't care any more. Inside herself she had a better life than them. Inside herself she could do anything.

And then Daphne came into her life. Daphne's parents had been killed in a train accident and she lived with an aunt and uncle who didn't like her. She and Daphne took on many roles in the letters they wrote and posted to each other. 'Have you heard from Edward yet?' 'Oh yes, he wrote me a wonderful letter. He wants to marry me but I'm not sure. After all there's still Laurence.'

'We should run away together,' Daphne said. 'Go to France and live with the Bohemians.'

Wanting

'Oh yes yes.' She could imagine those narrow streets and the sidewalk cafés and people who wore berets.

*

'I do not like that girl,' her mother said. 'She's a slut. I don't want you to see her any more.'

'But Mum...'

'She's a bad influence.'

'No she isn't. I love Daphne.'

'Love?' her mother screamed. 'The only one who loves you, and who will ever love you, is your mother. Don't you ever forget that. Your mother went through the most horrific pain to give you life. No-one knows love until they have been through that. Now come inside and have a piece of banana cake.'

*

'I want veal and mushrooms for dinner tonight, Mother,' she said when she went off to work on the knitting magazine where she did the layout. 'With baked potatoes and sour cream and maybe a salad with French dressing.'

'And I'll make a pavlova as well,' her mother beamed. 'And I've nearly finished the shawl you wanted.'

'Oh didn't I tell you, mother. I've changed my mind. I want a silk caftan.'

*

In the office they called him Junior because he was CR, the boss's, son. His wife was having a baby which Junior didn't want. She met him in the coffee bar downstairs by accident, and he told her all about it. She loved his brown eyes and the way his hair fell over his forehead. He was the first man she'd ever had sex with.

They did it on the floor in his office after work. She liked this better than food and told her mother she was working late and would get herself something in town.

After he'd zipped up his trousers and left her she would clamber to her feet, slip her panties from her ankles because there wasn't time to struggle with them, and follow him, watch him get on a Seatoun tram and go home to *her*. One day she got a taxi and went to the end of his road, paid the driver and walked up the road until she was opposite his house. She stood for some time watching it, seeing nothing until it got dark and the lights went on, the wife coming in and drawing the curtains.

*

She took to going there in the middle of the day so she could see the wife go outside to the clothes line or get in the car and go shopping. Then one day the wife wasn't there and Junior didn't come to work for several days. When he did, he was a different man. So happy. He brought the baby, Colin, to work and showed everyone, including her. His eyes didn't meet hers. She wanted to kill that baby and thought of many different ways that she could accomplish this.

*

Her mother was becoming worried. 'You've lost so much weight. Here let me make you a nice apple dumpling. You like those.'

'No, Mother. I'm not hungry.'

'What is the matter? Don't you love me any more? You haven't eaten at home for months.'

'Don't be silly, Mother. It isn't that.' She stomped off to the bedroom and closed the door.

*

Wanting 101

She learnt to drive. The instructor put his hand on her knee while he was teaching her but it wasn't him she wanted. When she had her licence she went to Junior's street every night and sat across the road watching his house. Sometimes she saw them inside. Sometimes just the two of them and sometimes only him smiling down at the baby. Once they had a party and she watched people going in and then coming out at the end of the evening.

*

'Where are you going every night?' her mother asked. 'Is it something so bad you can't tell your mother? I don't deserve this sort of treatment. After all I've done for you. No mother could have loved you like I have.'

'You're absolutely right, Mother.'

'Well then? What has happened to you? You aren't the girl you were. You've lost so much weight as well. Are you ill? Please tell me.'

'No, Mother. I'm not ill. Just leave me alone.'

'You never do anything with me any more. I feel so lonely. You haven't got a boyfriend, have you?'

'That doesn't deserve an answer.' She wanted to hit her mother, wipe that disgusting expression off her fat face, cut off her fat breasts.

'That's a relief. I'd hate to think you let anyone touch you... down there. You can't trust anyone these days, and there are so many diseases...'

'Shut *up*, Mother.'

'There's no call to talk to me like that.'

*

'What made you take the baby?' the woman in the white coat asked.

'He's my baby. What are you talking about?' Was there something wrong with this woman? Why did she keep asking such silly questions? The sun shone across the floor making a zigzag pattern. 'I went through horrific pain to give that child life. No-one could love him like I do. You don't know love until you have a child.' She thought of him asleep in his cot, his eyelashes like fans on his flushed little cheeks.

'He wasn't your baby, Adeline.'

'Oh go away you silly woman. I haven't time for you.'

She sat hugging her bony knees and thought of that pudgy little girl from so long ago, and the stupid mother who didn't have a life of her own. Poor twisted creature. What were they doing now. Maybe the mother had died and the girl had a family of her own? Maybe she had married Errol and they were happy ever after.

Commos

She used to envy a girl called Beverley because she had plain white knickers while theirs were the same as their dresses; Mum made them. No-one else had knickers the same as their dresses. Beverley had a young mother, too. Young and glamorous.

Katherine often wished she had a young and glamorous mother. One day Dad told them he'd been married before he met Mum. Only for a year, and she'd divorced him because they lived in a tent. Her name was Grace. She had long blonde hair and loved dancing. He showed them a photograph. Grace in evening-gown, standing, smiling. Mum had dark hair and hazel eyes. This Grace was blonde and blue eyed. She began to believe Grace was her real mother and that Mum had adopted her when she met Dad because Grace was too busy dancing and having a good time to bother with a baby.

Of course Katherine loved Mum and would never want to go back to Grace. But who could imagine Mum dancing and having a good time? A good time to Mum was talking about warmongers, the masses, dialectal materialism, and standing on a box in the street shouting at people: 'The workers must take over the means of production ...' When Katherine and her friends went to town on a Friday night she tried to avoid Allan Street in Courtenay Place but sometimes she couldn't, and there Mum would be standing up on her box surrounded by people who yelled horrible things at her. Mum called them hecklers and said she loved thinking of clever things to say to make them feel foolish.

No-one would have thought, if they hadn't known Katherine, that that was her mother up there. Katherine walked by as if there wasn't anybody there at all. And her friends never said a word. There weren't that many safe places to go on a Friday night. If they went near Cuba Street they'd be likely to see Dad selling the

Communist paper, *The People's Voice* and the trouble with him was that he was so friendly and would yell out, even if he saw them across the road. And it wasn't only Dad, there were other Communists they knew, too, who would talk to them. It was so embarrassing. To be a Communist was the worst thing you could be. Worse than being a leper. Everyone thought Communists were trying to take over the world, that they ate babies, cut people up and made them into meat pies. Katherine hated Social Studies or any subject where Communism might be mentioned. She tried to will herself not to go red but she always did. Even when the teacher might say something like, *the commonest form of something is ...* Katherine would still glow like a beacon. Maybe that was why she was the class clown, always making people laugh, never doing her work. And to make matters worse they had an unusual name. She knew as soon as she said it, people would say, 'Is your mother that Commo?' Katherine often planned to say 'Smith' but somehow she couldn't do it.

It was like living in two worlds, the inside one of the Communist party where she felt proud of her parents and the outside one of school and neighbours. She longed to have a mother like the other kids. Mum was different in just about every way. She did different things from the other mothers and she was a lot older. When they were young she would never tell her age and Katherine thought she was even older than she was! It wasn't until Mum was old enough to be proud that she looked *younger* than she was, that she told them she was thirty-nine when she had Katherine and forty-one when she had Marion. 'There could have been something wrong with us,' Marion said. 'We could have been Mongols.' They even felt lucky they were here at all because when Dad came back from the war he and Mum got single beds and never 'did it' again. They used to listen but they never heard any creaking or heavy breathing like the Summer kids did when their parents were in the bedroom with the door closed. Mr and Mrs Summer looked quite old too but they'd had lots of babies that had died so they must have done it a lot. Katherine and Marion were scared of Mr Summer because he had a bent back and was always yelling, 'Close the bloody gate' ... 'Maisie, Matthew! Come and help your mother!' Maisie and Matthew didn't hurry or seem to take any notice of him at all. All Mrs Summer said when he started yelling was, 'Oh Harold.'

Dad used to drive the trams. Katherine and Marion would take cheese and onion sandwiches, and tea in a milk bottle with a cardboard lid, down to the end of the road and wait for Dad's tram to come along. Then they'd get on it and stand in the front with Dad where passengers weren't supposed to stand. There was a little notice that said, *Please do not converse with driver.*

At the terminus in Miramar, Dad and his conductress would pour the tea into the cups Mum had packed, and open the cheese and onion sandwiches. Dad said onions were good for you. He rubbed onions into his scalp as well to stop him going bald, but it didn't make any difference.

The neighbours seemed to like Mum and Dad, even though *they* were Catholics and Mum and Dad were Communists. 'Just shows,' Mum said, 'that when people know one another there should be no disharmony.' When Dad came back from the war the neighbours even put a big banner across the road which said WELCOME HOME.

An Evening Out

'm totally devoted to you,' he sings as he finishes attaching his false eyelashes. The face stares back at him out of the mirror, aloof, beautiful, scarlet lips pouting. 'No doubt about it, Virginia,' he says. 'You're a knock-out.' She raises an eyebrow, mocking him. 'Come on,' he says. 'Lighten up a little.' She turns away and then looks back at him over her shoulder. Miss Untouchable Cool. He examines her from head to foot. That silver lamé covers her like the skin of a sinuous snake. Now for the silver earrings. He feels around in his flax kete until he finds the long dangling slivers of silver, tinkling and shivering as he puts them on. She steps back from the mirror. Oh yes.

Virginia puts her hand on the bed as she slips on her silver high-heels. As she stalks out of the room she kicks his greasy oil-stained jeans under the bed, feels her nose quiver. Filth. He is filth. This place is filth. There has to be something better.

The lemon meringue pie sits on the formica bench, a ghost of steam drifting upwards. He's a good cook, she has to say that for him. And then the cat, twisting itself around her legs. 'Call this devotion, do you, Marilyn?' she says. 'I know you're only after one thing.' She opens the fridge, presses her scarlet-tipped fingers to her chin in horror. Now she's going to stink of fish. Still, the cat can't starve. 'You'll have to have it on the bench tonight, darling, Mother can't bend down.'

She washes her hands with scented soap, wraps the pie in a clean tea towel, throws her silver lamé bag over her shoulder, trips along the hallway and out the door.

*

An Evening Out

Along his mother's path, wild flowers and grass. Summery smells. Hoping that Dora next-door is watching the television and not looking through the window. Opening the back door, shoving the pie on the bench. Calling, 'Mum I've just left the pie. See you tomorrow.'

'Come in, Joseph, I'm just watching the telly.'

'Can't Mum, in a hurry. See you tomorrow.'

*

Pulling open the stiff door of the Hillman Avenger, fitting herself inside, arms and legs with nowhere to go. Chugging up the hill to the university.

*

The dykes on the door look bored as they stamp her hand. The queen at the end of the table looks at her with envy, competitiveness, something.

'Virginia,' a tentative voice says.

She turns, looks down. 'Sheree, darling, you look wonderful.' Blonde, glistening, dewy red lips.

'Not a patch on you,' Sheree giggles. 'For a moment I thought I'd made a mistake.'

'My best creation yet,' she says. 'Even if I do say it myself.'

*

Faces look up at her as she sweeps through preening colourful men, and bland colourless women, to the dance floor. Stands there, feeling all eyes upon her and then she's off, *I am woman, I am strong ...*

Betrayal

When Larry told me he knew about David he also confessed that he'd been having an affair with Leanne for over a year. What could I do? I couldn't complain, could I?

It was all so civilised. Larry thought he and Leanne could buy the house next door. That way the kid's lives wouldn't be too disrupted. He said he'd come over and... you know.... see me. I wouldn't be without him really.

I was a mess. I wanted him back, especially since David had got the fright of his life and buggered off. I started walking around without any clothes on.

It was a strange time because Larry and I were still together. It was just that in the weekends he went out with Leanne.

I thought it could work, Larry coming over from next door. I really thought I could go along with it. I must have been mad.

After awhile I got angry. I got angry with Larry *and* David. They were both selfish bastards. I didn't need either of them.

I started going to a writing class. I wanted to write down everything that had happened so I could make sense of it all. I didn't tell Larry because it was none of his business. And that's when he went off his head. He came home one night and started accusing me of fucking David. He grabbed the phone book and searched for David's number. 'Hah,' he said, looking at me with raving madness in his eyes. 'Found it' He marched into the kitchen, grabbed the carving knife, opened his jacket, sliced open the lining and pushed the knife inside. Then he tore out of the house with me running after him. He swiped me across the face and jumped in the car. I ran back into the house. I'd never rung David at home before but I had to warn him. I was all fingers and thumbs as I turned the pages. At last I found Chalmers. There were two, both in Miramar.

Betrayal

David lived in Selwyn Street, the other in Bentley Ave. I stared at the D F Chalmers in Bentley Ave because the name and address had been underlined viciously with a blue pen. I clutched my chest, he'd got the wrong one.

    I never told the police about David. I thought I owed his wife that much. It turned out that poor Dudley Chalmers was gay. Unfortunately for Larry the police seemed to think it was a crime of passion, that Larry was a closet homosexual who'd killed his lover in a fit of jealous rage. Of course I didn't help matters when I told them that Larry had been behaving oddly for a number of years, that he often went out until all hours of the night and never told me where he was.

The Body

Hard to look back on those days when he'd been a lawyer, office, good suit. Now it was just him and Denis in this rabbit hutch of a house. Denis in the sun porch with an old blanket hanging down from the architrave, letting his stuff spread out into the living area. That was one thing about Denis that really pissed Dave off. *He* liked things to be clean and tidy. Shipshape.

He went out on to the deck, looked across the road to Kapiti Island snoozing like a huge monster in the bluegrey sea. Then something caught his eye down on the road. That fancy little homo was mincing along as if he owned the world. Dave wanted to pick up a rock, smash the queer little bastard's head with it. Who did he think he was? Then Val and the twins rolled up in their car and he thought better of it. He liked her. A woman who was decent, as far as women go. Good mother, kind to the kids, nice to Peter. What else could a joker ask for?

He'd had to go for that round-faced, curvaceous little bitch who'd taken the kids and buggered off. Broken his heart, that had.

He'd seen the boy once, appeared at the door one day, just like that. Good looking. Male version of her. They'd had a bit of a yarn. University student studying for a B.A. Not a drinker either, that had surprised him. But it meant he had a chance to do something with his life.

And that was it, never seen him again.

Dave sighed and went back inside. Tonight they were watching a video of the rugby he'd stopped himself from watching live because Denis was working. They'd kept away from everyone so they wouldn't know the score. Denis wasn't even going to the pub tonight so they could watch it. Dave didn't like going to the pub any more. Cheaper to stay home and caress his bottle of gin, think his miserable thoughts in private.

The Body

*

When Denis came home he put a carton of Lion Red on the table. 'Something smells bonza,' he said, as he disappeared behind the blanket.

'Banana cake,' Dave called after him.

'Quite the housewife, aren't yah?' Denis's nuggetty brown body streaked past Dave to the shower.

'Do you want your bloody face rearranged?' Dave yelled.

*

'Bloody won. Told yuh.' Dave lurched up, scattering bottles as he switched off the telly. He fell back on the couch beside Denis and watched him through a swirling mist as he threw another hunk of wood on the fire.

In the glow Dave could see the silhouette of Denis's face, all round and soft looking. He watched Denis put the bottle to his lips, tip his head back as he swallowed, could see the outline of his smooth throat.

Dave poured more gin into his glass, swigged it down and poured another.

When he looked at Denis again he was leaning back with his eyes closed, eyelashes like long black spider's legs, mouth pouty. His dressing gown had fallen open exposing knees and thighs, dark underpants. Dave felt his fingers creeping, as if on a mission of their own. They touched Denis's thigh, sidled on over and down into the warm groin area tangling with pubic hair. Then they snuck over the underpants and onto the soft mound of Denis's cock...

It was as if a whirlwind had hit the room. Things crashing, Denis's arms flailing around like a windmill. Dave felt himself being pulled up by the collar. 'Bloody fucking homo, that's what you are!'

'No, no,' Dave tried to say, as he clutched at Denis, trying to push him away.

'I'm outa here. Christ!' Denis swung away, letting Dave fall back on to the couch.

All Dave could think of was, that Denis would tell everyone, and he had to stop him. He reared up, grabbed a heavy hunk of wood, rushed after Denis and hit him over the head with all his might.

Denis crashed to the floor and lay there, blood oozing around his head.

Dave felt as if an electric shock had gone through him, making him stone cold sober. He dropped to his knees, scrabbled around, hands shaking, feeling for a pulse in Denis's neck. Nothing. He sat there, shivering, thinking no-one knows about this, there's only Denis and me here in this room.

Maybe he could cut the body up, put the pieces in the freezer, get rid of them in different parts of the country? But he couldn't face the idea of sawing through bone. It'd take bloody ages. And the gore...

He had to get Denis's body across to the beach, tip him off the wall. Lucky the tide was in. They'd just think he was drunk and had fallen in, yeah. He went to the front door, had a look out, not a sign of life anywhere. He went back to the body, rolled it over and pulled a sleeve off an arm, grunting and swearing, rolling him over to do the other, pulling the garment out from underneath him. Then he got his arms under Denis's arms and began to drag. Hell he was heavy, it was like trying to pull a carcass full of lead. He got him out into the small hallway, bumped, huffed and pulled until he was at the door. He was just getting it over the step when lights lit up the road. Bloody car coming. He dropped the body, jumped over it and stood back inside the house until all was clear again.

He was half way across the road when he heard another car in the distance. The thought flashed through his mind that he should

The Body

leave the body and flee, let it be run over but, then, that mightn't work. He had to get on to the bank above the beach before anyone saw them. With what seemed like superhuman effort he pulled and dragged, pulled and dragged until they were on the hard clay and shingle and he was falling down the slope. He scrambled up again, just as the car came roaring along the road. He flattened himself beside the body, hoping they hadn't been seen. When he looked up he could see his house, the nose bit lit up, eyes part darker. All the other houses in darkness, no-one watching.

He struggled up, tried to grab the body under the arms again but he kept slipping. Finally he pushed and off it went rolling down the slope until it stopped on top of the seawall. He slipped and stumbled after it, stood by it for a second looking down into the waves as they rushed up to the wall and away again. Then he sat on his bum, shoved the body with his feet and over it went like a roll of carpet. When there was nothing or no-one in sight he ran and crawled up the slope, whipped across the road and into the house, easing the door shut behind him. He was breathing and gasping, couldn't stop, full of terror now at what he had done.

In the living area he picked up Denis's dressing gown and put it in his room, seeing at the same time, in the dim light from the street light, the clothes Denis had been wearing dropped on the floor. Maybe he should get rid of them? What would the police think if they saw them? He scooped them up, grabbing Denis's wallet as well – better not have that around. He opened it quickly, saw some folded notes, grabbed them with fumbling fingers. Five twenties. Huh, Denis was always pretending he was broke. He put them in his pocket, went out to the kitchen, grabbed a rubbish bag, shoved everything in and then tipped the contents of the Kitchen Tidy on top of them. Back in the living area he collected the bottles, put them in the empty carton, took it out to the shed and dumped it with other boxes and cartons of bottles. Must get down to that recycling place tomorrow. Christ, tomorrow. What would tomorrow bring?

He was just picking chairs up, setting things in order again when he thought he heard a thump on the porch. He froze and then decided it was probably a possum. Then someone thumped and bashed on the door. The police! They'd found the body. Shit, that was quick. Dave felt as if he was going to die right there on the spot. The thumping started up again, louder, more desperate. He stumbled to the door, took several moments to open it because his hands were shaking so much. Finally he did it and there stood the ghost of Denis, pale and glowing.

'Oh, gawd all bloody mighty,' Dave shrieked, falling back against the wall and clutching his chest.

'Yeah yeah, I know.' Denis pushed past him and went into the living room, stood trying to warm himself by the dying embers of the fire.

Dave turned the light on, saw the bloody grazes on Denis's back and legs, waited for Denis to swing around and accuse him of attempted murder.

'I've done it this time,' Denis said.

'Wh ... what do you mean?' Dave sounded like a boy soprano whose voice had just broken.

'Some bastard must have caught me at it, that's all I can think.' Denis shivered.

'Wh wh wh what do you mean?'

'Could you get me dressing gown?'

'Yeah yeah. Okay.' Dave went behind the blanket, grabbed the dressing gown, saw blood on the collar. He opened the window and pushed it through, came out from behind the blanket. 'Can't find it, I'll get mine.' He whipped into his bedroom.

Denis was crouching by the fire putting paper amongst the smouldering wood, blowing on it to get it going.

Dave draped his dressing gown over Denis's back. 'I'll get you a hot drink,' he said.

In the kitchen he put on the jug and then flew out the back door, around the house, grabbed the dressing gown, rushed back to the

The Body

wash-house, shoved it in the washing machine with the other clothes and started it up.

*

'Here, instant coffee with a drop of brandy in it.' He handed the mug to Denis who was clutching the dressing gown around him and almost sitting in the fire.

'Thanks mate,' Denis looked up at Dave, his face was covered in blood and sand.

'Christ,' Dave said, 'you look bloody terrible.' When was Denis going to say something? Was he playing a waiting game, letting him suffer?

'This has been a real lesson, a real lesson,' Denis said more seriously than Dave had ever heard before.

'Yeah?' Dave quavered.

'Can't remember a bloody thing, just found meself hitting the water, don't know how it happened.' Denis shook his head.

'Really?'

'Some bastard must have caught me with his missus, that's all I can think. Why else wouldn't I have me clothes?'

'That's right,' Dave said. 'You've... ah... you're covered in blood.'

Denis put his hand to his head, then looked at the blood smeared all over it. 'Bastard must have given me one, that's why I can't remember anything.' Denis looked worried. 'Shit, there's someone after me and I don't know who it is' He took several more gulps of coffee. 'I don't even know if I fell into the water on me own, or I was pushed. It's eerie, he could be anywhere, waiting to get me, I'll never know.' He chewed at his bottom lip and frowned at Dave. 'Maybe I should leave town?'

'Might be a good idea,' Dave said, hoping to God Denis never got his memory back.

She's My Everything

Dogs are the only things you can trust. I've had my Marlene ever since I was eight and now she's seventeen, which makes her a hundred and nineteen in people years and me twenty-five.

Arnold, Mum's first husband, thinks I'm cruel, should put Marlene down but I aint gonna do that. She's happy. Wants to be with me, sit close when I'm watching the goggle box or surfing the net. I love her. Love's what keeps things alive. Too much hate and violence in the world. The world should have more dogs in it.

Sometimes I think Mum should die because she gets annoyed with me, thinks I order her around too much, getting too bent over and squashed up like an old man, she says. It would be better now if it was just Marlene and me. I have the dole. Could order pizzas. Share with Marlene. Marlene and me.

Me and Mum used to sit in the dark room with the white sun blazing outside when I was little, watching the goggle box. She didn't make me go to school and be pushed around by little screaming aliens. Mum was good then, didn't make me do things I didn't want to do, now she's getting mean.

*

Mum's rattling pots in the kitchen over the breakfast bar. I can see her. Wild face, thinks I should help her but I'm resting with Marlene. Mum's a mother, it's her job.

I have to eat at the table. I get up to please her, see the big grey sausages on my plate in grey gravy, green peas.

I expect Marlene to struggle up and come with me, creak creak, ache ache. But she's still on the floor, eyes closed. Funny.

She's My Everything

'Marlene,' I say. 'Uppsy daisy.' I bend down and prod her. 'Marlene, get up!'

Mum comes over. 'Oh dear.'

'No,' I say.

'Her time has come.' Mum looks sad.

'No no.' I run to the freezer in the washhouse, yank everything out, peas, sausages, chicken, meat. All on the floor, clunk clunk.

'What are you doing?' Mum yells, as I lay Marlene in there.

'Now she'll live forever,' I say.

The next day and the next day I take Marlene out, brush off ice and talk to her. My beautiful cold girl, put her back with food to eat in case she's hungry.

Mum gets Arnold to tell me I mustn't do this, that there's something wrong with me.

I don't like that. She's evil. The time has come.

Days of our Lives

A red station wagon drew up outside the BNZ and there was her dear son smiling and leaning over to open the door. She went out through the sliding glass doors, stuffed her bags and umbrella on the floor in front of the passenger seat and climbed in beside him. 'I really appreciate this,' she said.

'I didn't find the friend you were going to meet,' he said. 'I felt a real dick going up to all the lone men and asking if they were Trevor. They looked at me quite strangely.'

She laughed. 'Oh well, never mind, 'I'll just have to go to his work.'

'Who is this guy?' Stephen swung the car around in the direction of Wellington.

'I met him at Judith's birthday party. Remember, I told you.'

'Ah ahh,' Stephen glanced at her. 'The married man who's interested in your work.'

'Well, so he says.'

'You mean, you think there's more to it?' Stephen changed gear and roared out into the stream of traffic.

'Well, he does ring a lot and we do have such nice conversations.' She felt like a foolish schoolgirl.

'Oh, I see,' Stephen turned on the demister. 'He fancies you.'

'Well, I feel he does. I mean, why else would he talk so long? He's told me such a lot about himself.'

'I guess you'd know, Mum. I suppose he does talk about your work?'

'Of course. That's the excuse to ring. He keeps saying he's going to introduce me to this art dealer in Sydney so he can set up an exhibition there.'

'But it hasn't happened?' Stephen stared ahead at the road.

'I don't actually believe there is such a person. This talk has been going on for months with no sign of him.'

'Who's idea was it to have lunch?'

'Mine. I said I'd bring some photographs of my paintings. For the art dealer, you know.'

'Oh Mum.'

'And I've been punished for it, so you don't have to worry.'

'Eh?'

'God has intervened.'

'You don't believe in God.'

'Well, I feel *something* made my car break down, I honestly do. It was like that time with Sam. Something made him behave so uncharacteristically horrible, so I didn't go and live in the Wairarapa. What a disaster that would have been.' She watched the windscreen wipers swish back and forth, back and forth, and tried not to think about how much it was going to cost to tow the car to the garage and then find out what was wrong with it. The auto electrician who'd come to her rescue had shaken his head and looked serious. She'd already used her visa to buy clothes for this bloody lunch that had never happened and now... still she'd survived okay for nearly sixty years why should it change now. 'I'm not going to worry about the money,' she said. 'No point is there? Doesn't make any difference.'

'That's right,' he said.

In the changing room she'd been shocked to see the tyres of white fat bulging over her contained round stomach, - didn't seem that bad at home - and she'd thought, who'd want to go to bed with me? And then she'd thought the clothes would disguise the fat while she was on a diet. 'It's all for the best,' she said. 'It wasn't right.'

'I thought you didn't want anyone in your life,' Stephen said.

'I don't. Really, I don't.' It was watching *Days Of Our Lives*. All this stuff with Marlena and John Black had made her remember the excitement, the loveliness of love. Sometimes she nearly mentioned them to her friends, as if they were people she was close to. She'd just stop herself in time.

'Well, what were you doing this for?'

'I don't know. It's sort of been nice talking to him, feeling that I was attractive, you know.'

'You are attractive, Mum. I think you are.' He leaned over and touched her head with his.

'Yes,' she sighed. 'You know, when I was young I'd hear old people say they still felt the same as when they were young, and I didn't believe them. But it's true. I can't believe it when I look in the mirror and see my saggy neck.'

'You look great for your age.' He glanced at her.

'For my age. Yes... Oh, there's my poor old car.' She looked at her silver Mazda sitting on the island of muddy grass. 'I hate leaving her there but no-one can steal her, can they? She won't bloody go.' She felt strangely distanced from everything that was happening. Stephen here beside her, the rain, traffic streaming down the hill to the city. Trevor waiting.

She'd had it all planned, getting there early to find a park so she wouldn't be nervous and rushed, changing her shoes, leaving her raincoat in the car and just wearing her new jacket, doing her hair in the toilet, making sure there was nothing on her face that shouldn't be there, psyching herself up to be calm and casual. 'You've no idea how traumatic it was just stopping like that,' she said. 'Right at the lights with all that traffic behind me.'

'You're okay now.'

'I just sat there, turned on the hazard lights and waved people past.'

'How long did it take until that man came?'

'Only about three minutes, thank God. Was it okay to put that job off? I'd hate to have ruined things for you.'

'It's fine, I said I'd do it on Monday.'

'Why would anyone want to sacrifice their family?' she said. 'It would be so foolish.'

'His wife's probably gone off him.'

'Oh don't,' she said.

Days of our Lives 121

'Where were you going after lunch?'

'I'm collecting Susie from school for Amanda, then we'll go and have coffee. Tonight I'm going to the art awards. So you see, there was another reason for coming to town.'

Stephen turned, his blue eyes appraising her for a second before he turned back to watch the road. 'What were you going to do between lunch and picking up Susie? Go off to a hotel with him?'

'Really, Stephen!'

'Come on, admit it,' Stephen laughed. 'You were going to spend a couple of hours of wild passion in a hotel room.'

'That'll be the day.' She could see the two of them getting undressed, how ghastly. She wanted romance across a lunch table, wine, flirtation, the wondering. 'I've gone off the whole idea now. It's not right to go for someone else's husband. Why do I want to do that to myself? Or her?' She twisted her mother's wedding ring around her finger. 'No good can come from it at all, only heartbreak. I've known this all along.'

'You're an artist Mum, you can't have everything.'

'That's right. It's definitely off. I'm going to tell him.' She rubbed her hands together as if that decided it.

'Tell him what?'

'Not to ring me any more. I don't want it. I've been living in a dream world. He won't leave his wife.'

Stephen nearly hit the car in front. 'Leave his wife? Is that what you really want?'

'No. I don't know what I'm talking about.'

While Stephen double parked outside the building where Trevor worked she ran inside, still in her raincoat because it didn't matter any more. She stopped for a moment before she got into the lift and patted her hair in place and then floated up to the 5th floor.

'Is Trevor Austin here?' she asked the receptionist.

'What is your name? I'll tell him you're here.'

And there was Trevor welcoming her into his office. 'Elaine, what happened to you?'

'Oh it was terrible. I tried to ring, even sent my son.' She sat opposite him at his desk and thought how grey his hair was, not black as she'd descibed it to Stephen. 'My car broke down.'

'What a shame. I had such a nice surprise for you.'

'A surprise?' He was leaving his wife... He loved her...

He smiled, and she thought he really was such a handsome man. Maybe it was a good thing the car broke down because it made her behave more naturally.

'Gerald,' he said.

'Gerald?'

'My friend.' He smiled, waiting for her reaction.

'I'm sorry?'

'My friend from Sydney. The art dealer.'

'Oh yes. How stupid of me.' She tried to make herself sound enthusiatic.

'He came for lunch, so I wasn't on my own. He wanted to see the folder of your work. Still, I'll send them on to him. He had to get to the airport.' He glanced at her bag expectantly.

'Oh yes.' Thank goodness she'd remembered to bring them. At one point she'd imagined saying to him, 'I didn't bring them. It was you I wanted to see.' And he would have said, 'I didn't really want to see them.' And they would have looked at each other across the table and he would have reached across and taken her hand. Her makeup purse fell onto the foor as she pulled the packet from her bag. She put the photographs on the desk and bent to pick up her make-up. When she sat up again, feeling flustered, he was smiling as he looked at the photographs.

'These are so good. It's a wonder you haven't been discovered. But,' he smiled. 'I'm going to do it for you.'

He went on talking and smiling and saying something about Gerald coming back in November, and she smiled so much she felt the smile would be pasted on her face forever. This was what she'd been waiting for all her life and yet all she wanted to do was cry, get out of here and cry.

French Farce

It was just after midnight when we arrived at that hotel in Marseille. A hotel with no staff, remember? I felt sick with worry all the way from Heathrow. Something always goes wrong with me and numbers.

We each had a code to get into our rooms which were beside each other, down a narrow corridor. I couldn't wait to have a shower and fall into bed. Away from you.

I took out my pyjamas and towel, slipped off my shoes, put my glasses on the shelf by the small handbasin, put my money bag under the pillow, and went out into the hallway, making sure I had the code number in my pyjama pocket before I closed the door.

As I held my face up to the spray of water I thought about how I didn't have a home and would have to live with you until I found one. You, a needy old man, full of denial. Sometimes I felt like a dominatrix, the way you cried when I told you off.

I was pleased no-one was around when I returned to my room. I felt confident as I pressed the code number and watched the door begin to open. But I couldn't believe my eyes when a latch from inside slowly attached itself to a hook on the door frame. I tried to get my fingers through to free it. I repeated the code. Nothing happened.

'Oh no,' I wailed. 'This is a nightmare.'

A door up the hallway opened. A man poked his head out and abused me in French, then slammed the door.

I kept hitting, shoving and wailing as the door up the hallway opened again and abuse poured forth.

You came out in your pyjamas. 'What's the matter?' you asked.

'I can't get into my room.' I wept, trying to explain what had happened. But you got it all wrong and I yelled at you. There was no a way a thin piece of cardboard would help in this situation.

Then a door behind me opened and a man, dressed only in underpants, appeared. He pushed and shoved at my door with all his might.

You said we'd better get security and the three of us went down to the foyer where a group of people were smoking and talking. Someone pointed up some stairs and another man in underpants came out of a room and tried to push the door open. He went away and the first man gave one last shove and the door opened.

Later, you took my hand in yours and, with tears in your eyes, said how much closer you felt to me now.

I told this story at your funeral and everyone nearly fell out of their pews laughing. I said how your version of the truth was very different to mine. I said I hoped you'd be climbing mountains in the sky.

I didn't say how much I missed you.